This paperback edition published in 2020.
First published in 2019 by Flying Eye Books, an imprint of Nobrow Ltd.
27 Westgate Street, London E8 3RL.

Written by Stephen Davies and illustrated by Seaerra Miller,
based on the characters and storylines
created by Luke Pearson and Silvergate Media company.

1 3 5 7 9 10 8 6 4 2

Published in the US by Nobrow (US) Inc.

Printed and bound in Great Britain by Clays Ltd,
Elcograf S.p.A.

ISBN: 978-1-912497-59-1

www.flyingeyebooks.com

Based on the Hildafolk series of graphic novels by Luke Pearson

HILDA AND THE NOWHERE SPACE

Written by Stephen Davies

Illustrated by Seaerra Miller

FLYING EYE BOOKS

London | New York

N
E
S
CAMP SPARROW
CAMPSITE

CITY GATE
TROLBERG
SCHOO
HILDA'S HOUSE
FRIDA'S HOUSE
RIVER BJÖRG
DAVID'S HOUSE
BJÖRG FJORD

SPARROW SCOUT JOURNAL
TONTU
BALDY
HOUND

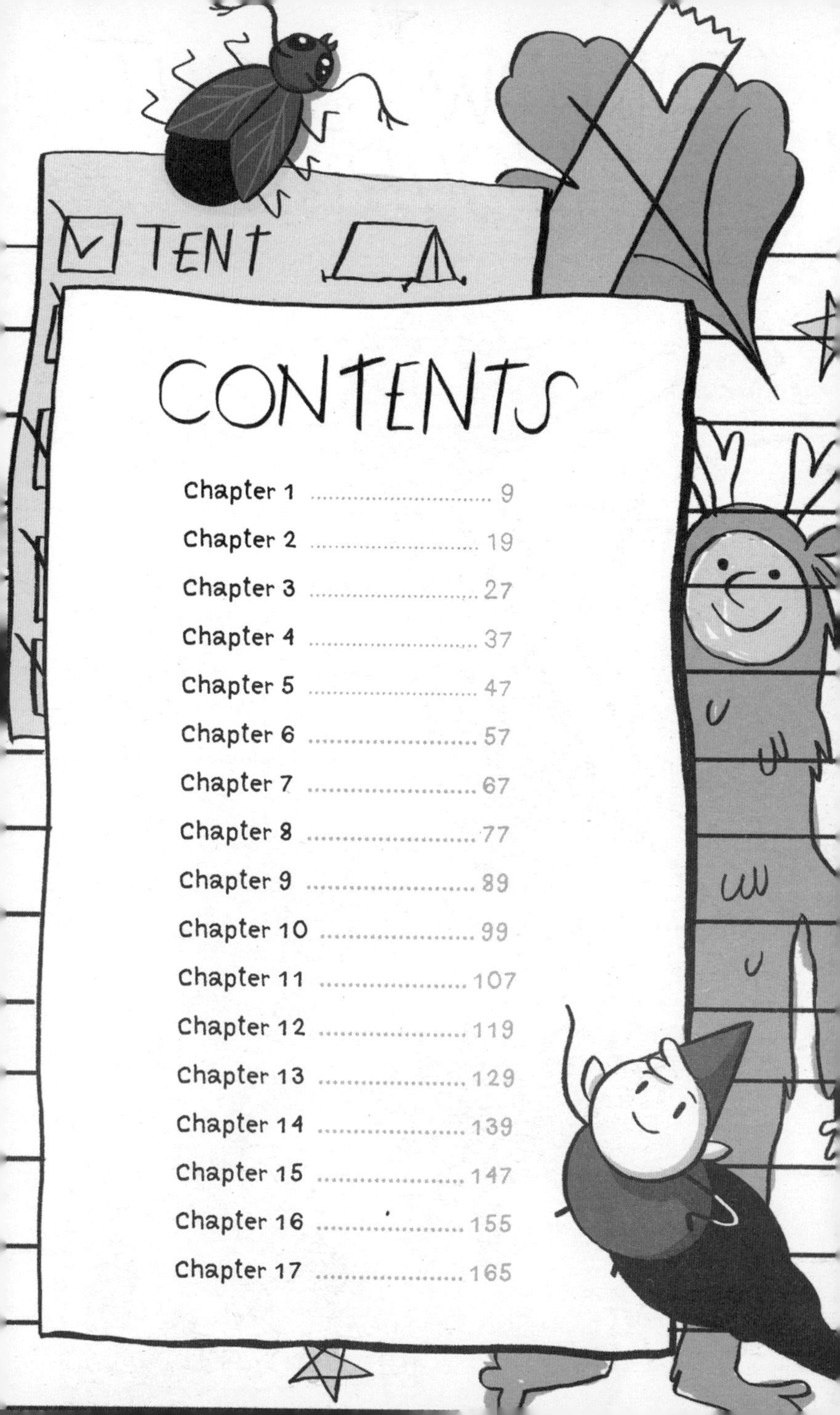

CONTENTS

1

Scooters scooted. Cars zoomed. Beetling along the sidewalk, hugging to her chest an enormous bag of cucumbers, a little girl with blue hair was heading home from the store. As she walked, her heart welled with excitement and she sang at the top of her voice.

"A-camping we will go,
A-camping we will go,
We'll pitch a tent and light a fire,
And dodge the hungry trolls!"

A pale boy trotted behind her with a bag in each hand and a bug on his head. At the mention of trolls, he paled even more.

"Hilda, *shush*," he hissed. "You shouldn't even joke about things like that."

"And you shouldn't worry so much, David," said Hilda. "Something traumatic could happen at any moment, but worrying isn't going to help." As she said this, Hilda stepped off the curb into the street, right in front of a bus.

"Hilda!" David darted forward and pulled her back just in time.

The bus screeched past Hilda's nose and knocked the grocery bag clean out of her arms.

Hilda fell backward onto the sidewalk and watched her precious cucumbers being pulverized by the tires of a hundred passing cars.

"It's OK," she said. "I've got plenty more in my satchel."

Just six months ago, Hilda and her mom had moved to Trolberg from their wilderness home, and Hilda was still struggling to get used to city life. The traffic was noisy and fast-flowing. The people were noisy and fast-flowing. Even the River Björg, running through the city, was noisy and fast-flowing. It was hard to find a moment of peace anywhere. One reason why Hilda was so excited about tonight's camping trip was that the campsite was situated in a large wooded area on the edge of the city. There, Hilda would at least be able to pretend that she was in the wilderness.

Hilda got to her feet and brushed herself off. As soon as the walk signal appeared, the two of them crossed the street and continued along the sidewalk with the Scout Hall on their right.

Hilda glanced up and saw the bright red Sparrow Scouts' flag fluttering at the top of the flagpole.

Joining the Sparrow Scouts had been Mom's idea, of course. Mom had been a Sparrow Scout when she was a kid and she loved the idea of Hilda following in her footsteps. Every Tuesday evening, when Hilda got back from the Scout Hall, Mom's first question was always the same:

"Have you earned any badges yet, darling?"

Hilda's reply was always the same, too:

"Not yet, Mom, but I'm sure I'll get one soon."

What she did not mention was that she had already tried and failed to earn twelve badges. She had gotten lost during her attempt at the Horseback Riding badge, and again in Orienteering, then again in Search and Rescue. She got burned in Cooking and accidentally cut her arm in Wood Carving. (She attempted to stitch the cut herself, hoping to earn her First Aid badge, but an ambulance arrived before she could finish.)

CHAPTER ONE

As soon as Hilda had left the hospital, she had signed up to do a Circus Skills badge and a Car Maintenance badge, but Raven Leader had taken her name off both lists and instead signed her up for Road Safety, Fire Safety, and three other kinds of Safety. Hilda tried her best for all five badges, but it turned out that safety of any sort was not her strong suit.

Hilda's last close call had been the Friends of the Park badge. For two whole days she had worked with her friends Frida and David to clear Gorrill Gardens of weeds, only to realize that the strange onion-like weeds were not in fact weeds but vittra, gentle bulb-shaped creatures hibernating in the summer sun. By the time Hilda realized the truth, the vittra had already been taken to the Trolberg Compost and Mulching Center and were being shunted along a conveyor belt toward the blades of the Big Chipper. Hilda, Frida, and David had to move fast to rescue the poor creatures before they were turned into mulch.

The rescue attempt succeeded, but the badge attempt failed.

None of that mattered now, of course. Tonight's camping trip would earn Hilda her first badge—the Camping badge—and after that anything was possible. Hilda smiled and sped up, playing hopscotch among the cracks in the sidewalk.

"Slow down," David grumbled. "We've been walking for miles. These bags are pulling my arms off. I don't know why we couldn't have brought our bikes."

"Walking's good for you," said Hilda.

"Not if your arms fall off mid-walk."

"My bike is brand new," said Hilda. "I don't want it to get dirty."

Hilda did not seriously believe that David would accept this excuse, and she braced herself for a sarcastic retort. None came.

When Hilda turned around she saw that her friend had stopped next to a newsstand. He was staring at the front page of the *Trolberg Tribune*, his face even paler than before.

DOCK HORROR! the headline shouted. BLACK HOUND SIGHTING AT TROLBERG HARBOR.

"Ignore it," Hilda said. "It's just a silly rumor made up to sell newspapers."

"Really?" David pointed at the photograph below the headline. "What's that, then?"

The blurry photo seemed to show a vast black shape crouching behind a shipping container.

"That's nothing," said Hilda. "It's just the shadow of the container."

"A shadow with ears?"

"Yes," said Hilda. "I mean, no. I mean, it was probably just a dead fly on the camera lens." She tugged at David's sleeve to move him on, but he stayed rooted to the spot, staring at the newspaper.

"This is terrifying," he said. "Do you think Raven Leader will cancel our camping trip when she sees the news?"

"Of course she won't," said Hilda. "We've been preparing for weeks."

"What if she does, though?"

Hilda swallowed hard. "If she does, I lose my last chance of a Sparrow Scouts badge, and Mom finds out at Friday's Badge Ceremony what a useless daughter she has."

"You think your mom will be disappointed if you don't win any badges?"

"Disappointed?" said Hilda. "No, she won't be disappointed. She'll be completely crushed."

On the corner of Hilda's street was a patch of scrubby crabgrass, and in the middle of the scrubby crabgrass sat a big round fuzzball with an enormous nose. Branches and leaves were stuck in its fuzz and its clothes were brown like dirt.

Hilda stopped. "Hello," she said.

The fuzzball raised its head and looked at Hilda. At least, it was probably looking at her. Its eyes were totally obscured by hair.

"Keep walking, Hilda," David muttered under

his breath. "Whatever you do, don't talk to it."

"I shall talk to whomsoever I choose," said Hilda. She turned back to the creature. "Good morning, Fuzzyface. Lovely weather we've been having."

"A little cold for me," the fuzzball replied. "But then, I'm not used to sitting outside. I've been banished from my house, you see."

"You poor thing!" cried Hilda. "Wait, what exactly are you?"

"What am I?" The fuzzball sighed. "I'm a restless soul, tossed on a sea of troubles, without a single friendly star to guide my course. That's what I am."

David pulled Hilda to one side. "It's a house spirit," he told her. "Otherwise known as a nisse. Nisses live inside people's homes and normally they're invisible. If this one has been banished, there's sure to be a good reason. It must have done something REALLY BAD."

"It looks hungry," said Hilda. "I think I'll give

it a cucumber."

"Don't," said David. "You shouldn't be talking to it, Hilda, and you definitely shouldn't start giving it cucumbers. House spirits are nasty little crooks, always telling lies to make you feel sorry for them."

Hilda could hardly believe her ears. "David, the Sparrow Scouts Oath says to be a friend to all people, animals and spirits, and to do a good thing every day. I'm going to give this house spirit a cucumber whether you like it or not, and then I'm going to see how else I can help it."

David shrugged and carried on walking. "Suit yourself!" he called. "I'll see you at the campsite later, unless that poor restless soul steals everything you own and shoves you down a well!"

As soon as David was gone, Hilda took a cucumber from her satchel and offered it to the house spirit.

The nisse accepted Hilda's gift without a word of thanks. "A cucumber without salt," it sighed, "is like a house without a house spirit—lifeless and dreary."

"We've got tons of salt at home," said Hilda. "Come with me, if you like."

Five minutes later, Hilda and the nisse were walking side by side up the three flights of steps that led to Hilda's apartment. Hilda loved making friends with magical creatures and learning their magical ways. So far, she had found out that her new friend's name was Tontu and that he used to live in a first-floor apartment near Bronstad Bridge. He kept trying to explain to her a thing called 'Nowhere Space', but however hard Hilda concentrated she could not understand it at all.

Hilda stopped at Apartment 5 and opened the front door. "Anyone here?" she shouted. "Mom? Twig?"

Mom was still at work, but Hilda's deer fox was very much at home. He flew out into the hall, yapping and snarling, a blur of white fur and jabbing antlers.

"Twig, calm down!" cried Hilda. "Tontu is our guest."

Twig stopped snapping at the nisse's ankles but continued to glare at him with obvious dislike.

"The living room's through there," said Hilda, pointing. "Go and make yourself comfortable and I'll get the salt."

Tontu went on through, but when Hilda entered with the salt shaker a moment later, the nisse was nowhere to be seen. Hilda looked behind the couch and under the table. She hunted inside the grandfather clock and all around Mom's drawing desk. She even climbed into the fireplace to peer up the chimney. Nothing.

"Tontu!" she called. "Where are you?"

A hand poked out from behind the bookcase and waved at her. Hilda stared. There was not enough space behind that bookcase for the nisse's nose, let alone for his big round body.

"Is that you, Tontu?" asked Hilda. "What on earth are you doing in there?"

"I'm perusing your Nowhere Space." Tontu's voice sounded strangely distant.

"Can you show me?" asked Hilda.

The hand disappeared and there was a long, awkward silence, as if the nisse was reluctant to invite a human being into Nowhere Space. But just as Hilda was about to give up hope, the hand reappeared and beckoned.

Hilda reached out and held the nisse's hand. She felt a short, sharp tug on her arm and a strange, falling feeling in her stomach. The living room swirled around her head and collapsed in on her like a broken umbrella.

3

Hilda found herself lying in a wobble-walled tunnel crammed with stuff. Strewn across the floor were coins, keys, checker pieces, grocery lists, batteries, hairbrushes, and dozens of pens missing caps. Piled up around the wobbly walls were school books, cookbooks, lampshades, sawblades, bulbs, cables, Christmas tree ornaments, and odd socks.

While Hilda was gasping and pinching herself, Tontu flung wide his arms and spun around like a ringmaster welcoming a crowd to his circus. "Welcome to Nowhere Space!" he cried. "The sum total of all the unused or forgotten spaces in your apartment. Every nook and cranny!"

Hilda looked around warily. "So everything that gets lost under the couch, or falls down the back of something . . . it all ends up here?"

"Exactly."

Hilda picked a beret off the floor of the tunnel. "I wondered where this ended up," she said. "And here's my math homework from last month! I told Miss Hallgrim it disappeared but she didn't believe me." She walked on, shaking her head in disbelief.

Tontu hurried to catch up to her. "Aren't you forgetting something?" he said, waving the cucumber at her.

"Here." She passed him the salt shaker.

The ceiling and walls of Nowhere Space were covered with strange, glowing holes. Hilda stood on her tiptoes to look through one, and to her amazement she found herself staring at the forest of coat hangers in her bedroom wardrobe. Another hole led to the utensil drawer in the kitchen, another to the tangle of wires behind the TV cabinet. Hilda stepped back down into Nowhere Space feeling strangely dizzy.

"Don't worry," said Tontu through a mouthful of cucumber. "You'll get used to it."

Hilda ran a finger across a dusty turntable record player. "This stuff can't all be ours," she said. "We've only been living here for six months."

The nisse shrugged. "Some of it probably belonged to the people who lived here before you."

"My brain is hurting." Hilda plunked herself down on an ugly brown armchair. "How on earth does an armchair fall down the back of a couch?"

"It doesn't. But if a thing is left unused or unloved for long enough, your house spirit assumes you're giving it to them."

Hilda stared. "You mean there's a . . . I have a . . . wait, we have a . . . ?"

"A house spirit of your own?" cried a furious

voice further down the tunnel. "Of course you do! Everybody does!"

Out from behind a broken vacuum cleaner stepped another big-nosed nisse. This one was completely bald and was wearing a yellow scarf and a red knitted sweater.

"Hey, that's *my* scarf!" cried Hilda. "And my second favorite sweater!"

The bald house spirit did not reply. It was glaring at Tontu, breathing hard through its nose.

It bent down, picked up a broom and charged.

Tontu made a dash for the nearest glowing hole, but the furious nisse swung the broom and tripped him up. Keys, coins, and capless pens jangled and crunched beneath them as they rolled over and over, grappling and scratching.

"Invade my Nowhere Space, would you?" snarled the irate house spirit.

"ARG . . . OOF . . . EESH," replied Tontu.

"Hey, Baldy!" cried Hilda. "Get off him!" She grabbed the end of the yellow scarf and pulled the spirits apart. "Can't we just sit down all together and— Hey, where are you going?"

Tontu had thrown himself headfirst through the glowing hole that led to Hilda's wardrobe. The bald nisse squirmed free of the scarf and dove after him in hot pursuit. Muffled fighting sounds moved from bedroom to hallway to living room.

Hilda hurried to the couch hole and poked her head up between two plump cushions. Right there in front of her, Twig, Tontu, and Baldy were chasing each other round and round the coffee table.

"Please, you guys!" yelled Hilda. "Violence never solved anything!"

The deer fox skidded to a halt, but the warring house spirits kept on chasing each other, littering the carpet with teaspoons, mugs, and coffee-table books.

Hilda thrust a hand up through the cushions and grabbed an arm of the couch. How many times had she plunged her hand down through this exact gap to hunt for a grocery list or a missing board game piece? Never in her wildest dreams had she imagined that she would one day squeeze a hand *upward* through the gap.

The house spirits dove behind a drinks cabinet and then tumbled out of the chimney into the fireplace. Twig blinked and fell over sideways. The nisse dashed across the couch, leaving sooty footprints all over the lime green cushions.

"HEY!" yelled Hilda. "YOU JUST STEPPED ON MY HEAD!"

Wriggling her body and hauling with all her might, Hilda inched herself out of Nowhere Space and up into a normal, sensible space. Like a butterfly from a cocoon she squeezed herself free, while the chase continued all around her. Into a cupboard and out of a drawer, in through a bookcase and out through a door, the two nisses showed no signs of slowing down. Trash cans flew. Shelves fell. A porcelain milkmaid shattered on the hearth.

"ENOUGH!" yelled Hilda.

Baldy was holding a moldy apple that he must have picked up in Nowhere Space. "Eat this!" he cried, hurling it at Tontu.

The apple missed its target and hit a framed picture of Hilda's mom on the wall beside the front door.

At that moment the front door opened and there in the doorway stood Hilda's mom. Hilda, Twig, and Tontu snapped to attention. Mom's picture dropped off the wall and smashed at her feet.

"What in the world has been going on here?" Mom's voice was low and menacing.

"Hi, Mom," said Hilda. "You're not going to believe this—"

Before Hilda could finish her sentence, Mom's gaze fell on Tontu. "GET OUT OF MY HOUSE!" she yelled.

"I'm gone," said Tontu, and out he went.

Hilda glanced left and right. Baldy was nowhere to be seen.

While Hilda swept and tidied the living room, she gabbed non-stop, trying to describe to Mom the mysterious science of Nowhere Space. “So?” she said, finally pausing for breath. “What do you think?”

Mom looked up from her dustpan and brush.

“I think you’re grounded for a week.”

“But—but—I can’t be grounded! If I don’t go on the camping trip tonight, I won’t get my Camping badge.” Hilda pouted and tried to make her eyes as big and cute as possible.

“You know that face doesn’t work on me,”

said Mom, but it was obvious she wanted the Camping badge just as much as Hilda did.

"Alright," she said at last. "You're not grounded. But from now on, I want you to focus more on badges and less on weird creatures. Is that clear?"

"Perfectly," said Hilda, hugging her.

When they had finished tidying up the living room, they went into the kitchen.

"I bought the cucumbers, like you asked." Hilda grabbed her satchel and tipped its contents onto the worktop. "I lost half of them in a bus-related incident, but I think these should be enough."

Mom gaped at the mound of cucumbers. "Yes," she said faintly. "Those should be enough."

The phone rang and Mom went to answer it. Hilda stayed in the kitchen and made an enormous pile of cucumber sandwiches.

"That was Raven Leader," said Mom, when she returned. "Three children have dropped out of the camping trip. Their parents got the jitters because they read some silly story in the newspaper. Something about a wild dog on the loose."

"The Black Hound?"

"That's right. Raven Leader thinks the story is a bunch of nonsense, and I agree with her."

"So she's not going to cancel the trip?"

"Of course not."

Hilda jumped for joy and went to pack her backpack. She found her equipment list and checked each item off as she put it in.

"Your backpack is almost as big as you are," said Mom. "Are you sure you can lift it?"

"Easy," said Hilda. She kneeled down, wriggled her arms through the shoulder straps, and leaned forward onto all fours, hauling the backpack up onto her back.

"You look like a tortoise. Can you even stand up?"

"I'll stand up in a minute," croaked Hilda. "I'm just catching my breath."

"Have you packed your toothbrush?"

"I don't need it. I'm going to use the split ends of a silver birch twig to brush my teeth tonight."

"I'll get your toothbrush," sighed Mom. "And a change of clothes, just in case it rains."

The campsite was a fifteen minute drive from home, on the outskirts of Trolberg. While Mom drove, Hilda read her new library book, *FORESTS AND THEIR UNFRIENDLY OCCUPANTS* by her favorite author Emil Gammelplassen. She had just reached a terrifying chapter entitled 'Thirteen

Reasons Why You Should Never Go Near A Hollow Tree' when Mom let out an ear-splitting scream.

Hilda jumped with fright and dropped her book. "Mom! What's the matter?"

Mom stopped the car and craned her neck, staring up at a rocky ridge in the west. "I thought I saw something." She blinked and shielded her eyes from the sun. "No, it's nothing. A blackberry bush, that's all. Sorry to startle you, Hilda."

"OK," said Hilda, but she did not go back to her book. She looked warily out of the window all the way to the campsite.

Camp Sparrow was in a forest clearing right next to the city wall, with the slopes of Mount Hár looming beyond. Linnets sang in the treetops. Crickets whirred and clicked in the long grass. A honey buzzard soared overhead.

"Such a peaceful spot," sighed Mom. "Reminds me of our life in the wilderness, before we moved to Trolberg."

Frida hurried toward the car, pointing at her

wristwatch. She wore an olive green safari jacket with dozens of button-down pockets. "Hilda, you're late," she said. "We need to get our tent up right now. We only have ten minutes before tent inspection."

Huffing and puffing, Hilda dragged her gargantuan backpack out of the car trunk.

"I'll see you tomorrow," called Mom from the driver's seat. "Enjoy yourselves—and look after each other."

In the middle of the campsite some logs had been arranged in a circle, with the tents beyond. The other scouts had already snagged the best camping spots, so Hilda and Frida pitched their tent on the edge of the clearing, next to the dark forest.

They had practiced putting up the tent plenty of times, so they both knew what to do. They staked down the corners of the groundsheet, erected the poles, and secured the guy ropes.

"Quick!" said Frida. "Hammer that last stake

into the ground. Raven Leader is starting to inspect the tents."

Hilda pulled the final guy rope taut. She placed the stake and swung her mallet hard.

"Ow!" An angry vittra popped out of the ground with the stake buried deep in its bulb-like head. "Yaroo!" it said, running away as fast as its tiny legs could carry it. The guy rope pulled taut and the vittra with the stake in its head continued to run on the spot, not getting anywhere.

The little bulb creature was stronger than it looked. The tent ropes twanged and groaned and some of the stakes popped right out of the ground, causing the whole thing to buckle and collapse.

"Poor creature," murmured Hilda. She grabbed the vittra around its middle, yanked the stake out of its head, and let it go free. The vittra shook a tiny fist at her, then turned and jumped down a hole.

"Tent inspection!" called Raven Leader, coming over to Hilda and Frida.

"Oh no," groaned Hilda.

Raven Leader stared at the mess of rope and canvas. She turned to the sheepish-looking girls. "I'm afraid it's a no from me," she said.

5

Tears pricked the back of Hilda's eyes. "What do you mean?" she said. "Have we failed already?"

"Not yet," said Raven Leader. "But one more mistake will definitely cost you the Camping badge, is that clear?"

Frida did a cheerful Sparrow Scouts salute. "Yes, Raven Leader. Thank you, Raven Leader."

"I don't want any trouble from you two tonight."

"No, Raven Leader."

"As soon as you've fixed your tent, go into the

forest and gather some dry sticks for the campfire."

"No, Raven Leader. I mean, yes, Raven Leader."

Raven Leader moved onto the next group. Hilda held the tent straight while Frida knocked the stakes back into the ground.

"You've got to admit, the vittra incident wasn't my fault," said Hilda.

Frida did not reply, but it seemed to Hilda that she was swinging her mallet more fiercely than before.

As soon as the tent was up, the girls ventured into the forest to gather sticks. They started off ankle-deep in thimbleweeds, but as the canopy thickened, the flowers thinned and disappeared.

"We should listen for woodpeckers," said Hilda. "Dead trees get infested with beetles, you see, and woodpeckers love beetles."

Sure enough, a tap-tap-tapping sound soon led them to a fallen tree where a woodpecker—a fine, black bird with a punkish scarlet crest—was busy eating beetles. "Mind if I join you?" said Hilda, beginning to wrench bits of dead wood off the tree. Before long her arms were piled high with logs and sticks for the campfire.

Frida was examining her compass, figuring out the best way back to camp, when she suddenly noticed a light through the trees. “Look, Hilda,” she said. “Someone has lit a fire in the forest. Let’s go and see who it is.”

They walked toward the light and came to a tiny campfire beneath a bludbok tree. Sitting by the fire was a fuzzball with a very big nose.

“Tontu!” cried Hilda.

Tontu looked up in surprise. “Oh, it’s you,” he said. “And now there’s two of you.”

“I’m not one of her,” said Frida hurriedly. “I can promise you that.”

Hilda went over to Tontu. “What are you doing out here?” she asked.

The nisse tutted. “I came out here because I thought I wouldn’t be bothered by people asking what I was doing out here.”

Frida tugged Hilda's sleeve. "Don't talk to it," she whispered. "I've heard that house spirits are nasty, lying—"

"Yes, I've heard that too," said Hilda. She crouched down by the fire and looked at where she imagined the fuzzball's eyes should be. "Tontu, are you OK?"

Tontu lifted his head. "Nipped by cold and gnawed by hunger. Otherwise, peachy keen."

"Why don't you go down into Nowhere Space?"

"Because I'm outside. Going into Nowhere Space when you're outside is incredibly dangerous."

"Why?"

"Have you ever heard of the Ehrenfest Paradox?"

"No."

"Then you wouldn't understand."

Frida was getting impatient. "Come on, Hilda. We need to get back to the others. They'll be wondering where we are."

"Just a minute," said Hilda.

Frida suddenly realized what her friend was doing.

"Hilda, that's our wood! We just spent ages collecting it. Let him gather his own wood if he wants to get warm."

Hilda ignored her and carried on building a pyramid of sticks around Tontu's flickering flame. When the fire began to properly blaze, she positioned three big logs with their ends poking into the flame.

"There," she said, straightening up. "That'll keep you warm for an hour or two. And I've got loads of cucumber sandwiches in my rucksack back at camp—nice and salty, just how you like them. I'll bring you some later."

Hilda and Frida hurried back to the dead tree to replenish their wood, and then went back to camp. Soon, they were sitting around the campfire with the other Sparrow Scouts, eating their sandwiches and sipping hot chocolate from enamel mugs.

"Time for some scary campfire songs!" cried one of the chief scouts. He picked up his guitar and led everyone in singing *Rat King in the Harbor* followed by *Way Down Yonder in the Huldrawood.*

David came over and sat next to Hilda. He was pretending to enjoy the songs, but Hilda could tell how frightened he was.

Hilda raised her hand to request the gentle song *Did You Ever See a Giant go This Way and That?* but the guitar player ignored her and started singing another scary one. This time it was a song he'd made up himself called *I'm Being Swallowed by a Big Black Hound*.

The children laughed themselves silly at the new song, except for David, of course, who had to lean forward onto his knees to stop them from shaking.

"Oh no, oh no,
It's swallowed my toe . . .
Oh gee, oh gee,
It's up to my knee . . ."

"This is going to give me nightmares," David whispered to Hilda.

"Try to enjoy yourself," she whispered back. "You know it's just a song, right?"

"I know." David looked like he was going to cry. "The truth is, Hilda, I've had nightmares every night this week. I don't know how to stop them."

"Oh fiddle, oh fiddle,
It's up to my middle . . .
Oh heck, oh heck,
It's up to my neck . . ."

"What sort of nightmares?" Hilda whispered.

"Tunnels," said David. "Rat kings. Salt lions. Trolls. That sort of thing."

"Oh dread, oh dread,
It's swallowed my—"

The children all gave a loud gulp and fell over laughing.

"That's about enough nonsense for one evening!" Raven Leader chuckled. "Time for bed, everyone."

The scouts groaned in disappointment, but they were eager to earn their Camping badges so nobody complained. They lingered around saying goodnight to each other, and soon the sounds of toothbrushing and toothpaste-spitting mingled with the soft *churr* of crickets in the undergrowth.

Hilda got ready for bed and wriggled into her sleeping bag.

"Goodnight, Frida," she whispered.

"Goodnight." Frida sounded cheerful. "Well done, by the way."

"Well done for what?"

"For earning your first badge," said Frida. "All you have to do is sleep right through till morning and the Camping badge is yours."

"Oh, yeah," said Hilda. "Easy."

But even though Hilda desperately wanted that badge, she had no intention of sleeping through till morning. She had a promise to keep. At the foot of her sleeping bag was a box of cucumber sandwiches that needed to be delivered to a hungry house spirit deep in the forest.

6

Clutching her compass, flashlight, and sandwiches, Hilda crept out of her tent and ran, half crouching, into the forest. She switched on her flashlight and walked in a southwesterly direction, trying not to snap any twigs underfoot. She mustn't wake the sleeping Sparrow Scouts.

Hilda paused. Was Tontu's camp southwest or southeast? She had thought it was southwest, but she was no longer sure. The branches in the beam of her light looked strange and twisted,

like monstrous tentacles. Dark hollows gaped on every side. Hilda wished that Twig was with her. She wished also that she had never laid eyes on Emil Gammelplassen's *THIRTEEN REASONS WHY YOU SHOULD NEVER GO NEAR A HOLLOW TREE.*

Suddenly she saw a flicker of light through the trees. *Tontu!* Hilda picked up her pace, brushing aside the spindly branches that reached out to bar her way. The clearing was just ahead. How happy Tontu would be to be given such a big pile of cucumber sandwiches, not to mention a paper bag of hazelnuts and rowanberries.

Hilda was just about to step out into the clearing when she heard a voice. The voice and the words it spoke made her blood run cold.

"*As David's head fell off his body and tumbled screaming down the mountainside, he realized that his head was bouncing directly into—*"

Hilda sprang back in horror and crouched down low behind a bludbok stump. Goosebumps prickled on her neck and arms.

"His head bounced into what?" said another voice. "Into a vittra tunnel? Into a witch's cauldron? Come on, tell us!"

Hilda slowly raised her head to peek over the top of the tree stump. In the open space before her, a dozen teenage girls were sitting cross-legged around a campfire. They craned forward to listen to the speaker, eerie firelight illuminating their chins and cheekbones.

The speaker flashed an evil grin that seemed to crack her face in two. "His head," she whispered, "bounced into the mouth of yet another troll!"

"Awesome!" cackled another voice.

"The perfect nightmare," said another.

"Aha ha ha, you're the wickedest marra ever!"

What's a marra? Hilda wondered. I've never heard of such a thing.

The teenagers' campfire crackled and popped. Green and purple shapes appeared within the flames. Monstrous creatures. Clawed fingers. Wide, staring eyes.

"What happened next?" a stringy-haired girl piped up. "Did this David kid wake up?"

"No." The speaker grinned. "He just thrashed around in his sleep, making little moaning noises, like this." The teenager rolled her head from side to side and whimpered softly, to the delight of her companions.

Hilda's blood boiled. David had been having nightmares for weeks, and somehow this girl was responsible. What kind of dark magic enabled a human girl to create bad dreams for other people?

Hilda placed the compass, flashlight, and sandwiches on the grass beside the tree stump. She dropped to her tummy and crawled forward through the long grass, trying to get a better look at the speaker. There was something strange about that girl, something about her eyes . . .

The speaker lifted a hand to call for silence. "Enough about last night," she said. "Last night is old news. Last night is history. Tonight, I intend to give young David a nightmare of such brainboggling horror that he will be afraid to . . . ever . . . close . . . his . . . eyes . . . again!" She widened her eyes in mock fear and at that moment Hilda noticed what was odd about her. Her eyes glowed a ghoulish green.

The green-eyed girl pointed eastward to a gap in the forest canopy, where a silver-edged cloud was drifting across the sky. "Nice night for a nightmare," she proclaimed to her companions. "Look, the moon has risen!"

The cloud drifted away and there in the sky above them was the biggest full moon Hilda had ever seen, a huge luminous pearl hanging in the heavens.

So beautiful, thought Hilda.

And then, to her horror, she realized that she hadn't thought it. She had said it out loud.

Thirteen ghastly faces turned toward her Hilda pressed her body flat against the grass. She squeezed her eyes tight and held her breath. Moments passed.

"Duh!" cried a gleeful voice. "Just because your

eyes are closed doesn't mean we can't see you. It doesn't work like that."

Hilda opened one eye. The grass around her—the whole clearing, in fact—was bathed in silvery moonlight.

"Is it, like, a trick of the moonlight, or is her hair actually blue?" said another voice.

Light-headed and sick with fear, Hilda stood up and faced the ghastly group. "I heard what you were talking about," she said, her voice trembling. "I heard it all, and I think you're . . . I think you're very mean."

The nightmare girls jeered and cackled. They got to their feet and advanced toward Hilda, grinning horribly.

"Go away," quavered Hilda.

To Hilda's amazement, they did exactly that. They stopped, stared at her with big round eyes, and vanished into thin air.

Hilda stood there, stunned. Wow, she thought. I've never had that effect on people before. Perhaps those girls caught a glimpse of my inner strength. Perhaps they realized they'd met their match.

Hilda smiled to herself and brushed a leaf off the front of her sweater. This must be what they call a coming-of-age moment, she thought. If I can stare down thirteen evil teenagers, I can face anything.

Something moved behind her. Hilda turned round and instantly she understood the real reason why the nightmare girls had left in such a hurry. There before her stood the biggest, blackest, most monstrous beast she had ever seen in her life. Its eyes blazed red in the moonlight. It drooled. Its sinews quivered, preparing to pounce.

"AAAAAAAH!" screamed Hilda. "IT'S THE BLACK HOUND!!!"

7

The Black Hound bent down toward Hilda, nostrils flaring. Then it opened its jaws and leaped forward.

Hilda was ready for it. She dove to the ground, rolled underneath the belly of the beast, and staggered to her feet on the other side. She snatched up her snack box and scattered its contents all over the ground.

"Here you go!" she cried, as the beast

whipped round to face her. "I hope you like cucumber sandwiches."

The Black Hound wolfed the sandwiches in ten seconds flat, then turned its attention back to Hilda. It advanced toward her, licking its jaws and growling deep down in its throat.

Hilda turned and set off running through the forest. She no longer had her compass and she had no idea which direction she should go in. Orienteering had never been her strong suit.

The hound galloped behind her, gaining on her with every stride. There was no way she could outrun it. It was nearly upon her. She could feel its putrid, meaty breath on the back of her neck.

It's over, thought Hilda. Goodbye, sweet world.

And then out of the corner of her eye she spotted a hollow bludbok tree.

Hilda did not hesitate. She dove into the hollow of the tree and cowered in the darkness. Emil Gammelplassen would have disapproved, but Emil Gammelplassen had never been chased

by a bloodthirsty monster as big as a bungalow.

The hound bared its claws and raked the bark of the bludbok tree. It shoved its muzzle into the hollow as far as it could and snapped around in rage. Hilda could feel at least three creepy-crawlies climbing up her leg, but she didn't care. The only thing she cared about right now was staying as far away as possible from the slobbering jaws of the hellhound outside.

She waited in the hollow for what seemed like hours. What time was it? she wondered. Midnight? Had the Black Hound gone away?

At long last she decided to make a run for it. She clambered out of the tree. She tiptoed away. One step. Two steps. Three steps . . .

A twig snapped close at hand.

Hilda gulped. The hound had tricked her. It had been lying in wait for her to emerge. She turned to dash back to the hollow, but she tripped over a tree root and sprawled on the forest floor.

"Don't eat me!" Hilda shrieked, covering

her face. "I'm not ready to die! I don't have any badges yet!"

"You certainly don't," said a familiar voice. "And if you think you're getting your Camping badge after this foolish escapade, you're as wrong as wrong can be."

Hilda squinted up into the beam of a flashlight. "Raven Leader!" she cried. "I'm so glad to see you. And Frida! You're here too?"

"Yes, I'm here," said Frida, "and I just want to reassure you that you're safe now, Hilda. Your ordeal is over. You'll be fine."

Raven Leader shone her flashlight on Hilda's dirty, disheveled clothes and hair. "What happened to you?" she gasped.

"The Black Hound!" cried Hilda. "I saw it. It chased me. It's somewhere in the forest."

Raven Leader stared at her. "If you're making this up—"

"I'm not, I swear."

"Hound or no hound," said Frida, "everything is

going to be alright, I promise."

Hilda frowned at her. "Frida, why are you talking funny?"

"I'm earning my Emergency Aid badge," said Frida. "I noticed you were gone, I raised the alarm and now I'm reassuring the victim at the scene of the emergency."

"Well, stop reassuring me," said Hilda. "It's creepy."

An eerie canine howl split the air. It was impossible to tell how far away it was, or in which direction.

"On second thought," said Hilda, "you can keep reassuring me—to get your badge, I mean."

Raven Leader led the way back to Camp Sparrow and began an emergency evacuation. While the dazed scouts took down their tents and packed up their backpacks, Raven Leader called their parents to arrange lifts.

"None of this is your fault," Raven Leader told the scouts, "so don't worry, you will still get your

Camping badges."

A sleepy cheer filled the air.

"Except for one of you," she added, glancing at Hilda.

The following afternoon, Hilda met Frida and David at the Trolberg Municipal Library. David was yawning and he had dark bags under his eyes.

"More nightmares?" asked Hilda.

"Worse than ever," said David. "You said on the phone that you might know what's causing them."

"I do," said Hilda. "Your nightmares are being caused by some . . . girl!"

SLAM! A heavy book landed on the table between them. Hilda looked up and saw the librarian standing on a wheeled ladder high above her.

"You're welcome," smiled the librarian, shoving herself off and rolling away down the aisle, black cape flying behind her.

Hilda looked down at the book in front of them. The title was emblazoned in gold lettering on a plain black background: *Tales of the Marra.*

"Yeah . . . that," muttered Hilda.

They flipped through the pages of the book. It was full of pencil illustrations of stringy-haired girls similar to the ones Hilda had seen in the forest.

"*The marra are nightmare spirits,*" Hilda read. "*They visit sleeping humans at night and create nightmares out of their fears.*"

"Look," said Frida. "It says here that the marra will pass over you if you strap yourself into bed with a leather belt."

"No way," said David. "I'm scared of leather belts."

Frida turned a page and continued to read. "It says the marra waits until you're asleep, enters your room through the keyhole, hovers above your bed, and delivers your nightmare. Ugh, this book is enough to give anyone bad dreams."

Hilda chewed her lip. An idea was coming together in her mind, an idea so crazy it just might work.

"Hey, David," she said. "Is there a tree outside your window?"

"No."

"A drainpipe?"

David nodded. "Yes, I'm pretty sure there's a drainpipe."

8

Mom laughed when Hilda asked if she and Frida could sleep in the tent again that night. "You've really got the camping bug, haven't you?" she said.

Frida's parents also agreed to the sleepover, so after dinner the girls went ahead and pitched the tent in Frida's backyard. When Frida's mom came out to say goodnight, she found the two friends tucked up snuggly in their sleeping bags.

As soon as Frida's mom went back inside the house, Hilda and Frida unzipped their sleeping

bags and sat up, fully dressed. Hilda shone her flashlight onto Frida's clipboard and read her plan through one last time.

PLANS FOR DEFEATING THE MARRA

H = Hilda F = Frida D = David

A = Alfur M = Marra

7:30 H & F Creep out of H's tent and go to D's house

7:35 D climbs down drainpipe and goes to wait in H's tent

7:37 H&F climb up drainpipe and enter D's bedroom

7:40 H ties tiny hammock to door handle

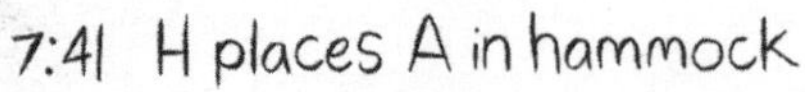

7:41 H places A in hammock

7:42 F goes to sleep in sleeping bag under desk, strapped in with leather belt

7:43 H goes to sleep in D's bed
?:?? M enters D's room through keyhole, knocking A out of his hammock onto the floor
?:?? A wakes F
?:?? F lassoes M with leather belt
?:?? H gives M a good talking to
?:?? M cries and promises to be good
?:?? H, F, D, A, and M live happily ever after

By the time they finished reading, Hilda was smiling all over her face and Frida was scowling like a crinkly dog.

"It's far too complicated," Frida complained. "Too many things that could go wrong."

"Stop worrying," said Hilda. "Alfur doesn't think the plan is too complicated, do you, Alfur? Do you, Alfur? Alfur, are you there? You like my plan, don't you, Alfur?"

The elf in Hilda's ear cleared his throat hesitantly. "It's the only plan we have," he said at last.

Frida did not look reassured, but it was already seven thirty and time to get going. The girls crept out of the tent and wriggled through a gap in the hedge onto a darkened street.

"This way," whispered Frida. "Follow me."

Soon they were standing in front of David's house, looking up at his bedroom window. At seven thirty-five on the dot, he opened his window and slithered down the drainpipe, landing softly on the sidewalk next to them.

"Thanks for this," David whispered. "Good luck with the marra."

When Hilda had lived in the wilderness with her mom, she had spent lots of time climbing trees, and this drainpipe was just like the smooth trunk of a maple tree. Hilda positioned her hands behind the pipe, pressed the soles of her shoes against the wall, and clambered all the way up to the window in thirty seconds flat. Frida followed, and they helped each other through the window into David's room.

Hilda took from her pocket a tiny homemade hammock and tied it to the door handle, level with the keyhole. "Make yourself comfortable, Alfur,"

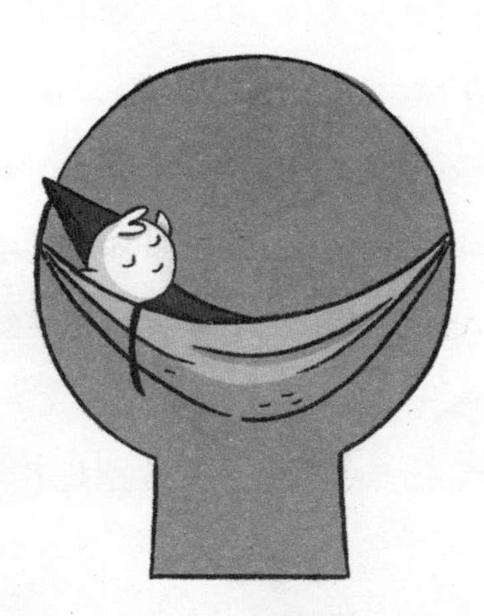

she said, laying the elf gently in the hammock. "Are you sure the marra won't see you?"

"Positive," said Alfur. "No nightmare spirit has ever signed an Elf Visibility Form, and we intend to keep it that way."

David's sleeping bag was under his desk. Frida climbed inside and strapped herself in with a leather belt. Hilda turned out the light, climbed into bed, and pulled the covers over her head.

"So far, so good," whispered Frida. "Sweet dreams, everyone."

Hilda closed her eyes, nestled her head into the pillow and did the same as she always did when she wanted to get to sleep fast. She pictured her old home in the wilderness, a little red cabin surrounded by snowcapped mountains. She pictured forests and plains, waterfalls and rivers. She pictured herself running under an infinite blue sky, her adventuring satchel tight against her back and her trusty snow-white deer fox bounding at her heels.

"Dear old Twig," she murmured. "I'm so glad

you're with me."

The deer fox looked up and snarled at her. Hilda gasped. Twig's eyes glowed green, just like the girls she had seen in the forest.

"AHA!" said Frida's voice. "Got you!"

Hilda sat up in bed and flipped on the bedside light. The marra was hovering in the air above her. Their eyes met and the evil grin on the marra's face transformed into astonishment.

"You're not David!" the marra cried. "You're that girl from the forest. What are you doing in David's bed?"

"Tricking you," said Hilda, pulling back the covers. "And now we're going to have a little chat."

The marra tried to flee, but she did not get very far. Alfur had woken Frida, exactly as planned, and Frida had tied the leather belt around the nightmare spirit's ankle. The other end of the belt was tied firmly around a bedpost.

The marra screeched in fury. "Let me go! I can't stand the feel of leather on my spirit skin!"

"Shush," said Hilda. "We'll let you go in a minute,

once you've promised to stop giving David nightmares."

"No way," said the marra. "The girls love David's nightmares, and so do I."

"But he finds them very upsetting."

"Cool."

"You're ruining his life."

"I know."

"But"—Hilda glanced at the clipboard on the bedside table—"this is where you're supposed to cry and promise to be good."

"Sorry, not sorry." The marra grinned.

Hilda and Frida exchanged a look. They needed a new plan fast.

Hilda unbuckled the belt from the foot of David's bed. "You're right," she sighed. "You should probably keep on giving David nightmares. He's about your level."

"My level?" The marra frowned. "Are you dissing me?"

"Of course not." Hilda untied the belt round the marra's ankle. "I'm just surprised you don't choose a more challenging victim, that's all. You know why your friends in the forest were laughing last night, don't you?"

"Sure. They were laughing at David's head falling off and bouncing down the mountain into a—"

"No, they weren't. They were laughing at you, because you always choose the same easy target. It's simple to scare a scaredy-cat, right?"

The marra's eyes flashed. "Zip it, kiddo. What I do isn't simple."

"If you say so." Hilda smiled. "You're free to leave, by the way. Keyhole's that way."

The marra did not leave. She stayed where she was, hovering above Hilda, scowling and stuttering.

"You want me to choose a more challenging target? Really? Is that what you want? Well, how about I choose YOU, kiddo? How about I unleash a sweet little nightmare into YOUR tiny brain?"

Hilda shrugged and yawned.

"You could try, I suppose. On one condition."

"What's that?"

"From now on, you leave David alone."

9

Hilda lay back down in David's bed and closed her eyes. She pictured herself running under an infinite blue sky, her adventuring satchel tight against her back and brave little Twig cavorting at her heels. She pictured herself running among the foothills of Boot Mountain toward a little red cabin in the west. Orange light shone from the cabin's windows. Mom must have lit a fire in the hearth.

"Hi, Mom, I'm home!" called Hilda, barging in through the front door and pulling off her boots. The house was toasty warm, and a divine aroma of ginger, nutmeg, and caraway seeds wafted over her.

"Hilda!" Mom jumped up from her desk.

"You've let the spiders in!"

Hilda looked back at the open doorway. An army of tarantulas poured in through the door and spread out across the wooden floorboards. Some swarmed up the legs of the dining-room table. Some crawled across the couch and the TV screen. Some clambered up Hilda's jeans and sweater.

"It's alright, Mom!" Hilda grabbed a jar and started scooping furry spiders into it. "I can use these for my bug collection! Maybe I'll get a Sparrow Scouts badge."

Mom's strange, luminous pupils dilated in surprise. "You're not frightened of tarantulas?"

"Not really," Hilda replied. "They're cute, in an ugly sort of way."

Somehow Hilda managed to scoop all of the spiders into a single jam jar. She labelled the jar *TARANTULAS* and took it upstairs to her bedroom. "I told you I'd be a more challenging target," she whispered.

Twig was sitting on the bedroom windowsill,

growling softly. He was not looking at the tarantula jar. He was looking at something outside. He pawed the windowpane and his tail began to quiver.

"What's wrong, boy?" Hilda said. "What can you see?"

She opened the window and leaned out. As she did so, a huge hand grabbed her round the waist. She felt herself being dragged out of her bedroom and up into the air, her legs dangling helplessly beneath her.

"Mmmm," said a deep voice. "You'll make a delicious snack."

Hilda looked up and saw a forest giant with glowing eyes.

"That's odd," said Hilda. "In his book *FORESTS AND THEIR UNFRIENDLY OCCUPANTS*, Emil Gammelplassen seems certain that forest giants don't eat people. Are you trying new things because your life's in a rut? Do you want to talk about it?"

She wriggled out of the giant's grasp and clambered up to its face to get a closer look.

The giant's eyes were like green-tinted glass. Through them, Hilda could see the teenage girl staring right back at her.

"What scares you, crazy girl?" The teenager narrowed her eyes and glared at Hilda, before the giant seized her in its enormous fist and threw her away from itself as hard as possible.

"*WHOA!*" cried Hilda as she hurtled through the air. "*OOF!*" she howled as she landed on the back of a passing woff.

There was something odd about the woff. Even while riding on its back, Hilda could see a radiating glow coming from its eyes.

"Interesting," said Hilda out loud. "*Whoa-oof* sounds a bit like *woff*. Is that where the word *woff* comes from? I bet it is!"

The woff went wild, soaring and bucking. Hilda wrapped her legs around the beast and clung onto its neck fur, giggling helplessly. Then she leaned forward and whispered in its ear, "Is this really the best you can do?"

The infuriated woff turned its nose downward and plummeted like a stone toward the ground.

"Crash landing!" whooped Hilda, but the woff pulled up at the very last second. Its tummy fur skimmed the surface of the River Björg and it accelerated once more, rocketing toward the city of Trolberg.

"Hilda! Is that you?"

Hilda looked to her right and saw Frida riding her bike along the west bank of the river, pedaling hard and waving happily.

"Hilda! Over here!"

David was riding his bike along the east bank of the river. It was definitely David, except that his face was tanned and the bags under his eyes were gone. He leaned low over the handlebars of his bike, looking perfectly healthy and fit.

Hilda waved at her friends.

"Get off the woff, you dingus!" yelled Frida. "We don't ride woffs in Trolberg, we ride bikes."

"That's right," laughed David. "The street doesn't have a woff lane!"

Hilda shook her head and clung on even tighter to the woff. But the moment they passed over the city gates, the woff between her legs transformed into a brand-new bicycle.

Frida and David cheered as Hilda's bike plummeted to earth and landed upright in the bicycle lane of Trolberg Main Street. Hilda tried to pedal in a straight line but she lost control, hit the curb, somersaulted over the handlebars and sprawled on the sidewalk.

"Can't you ride a bike, Hilda?" Frida shouted.

"Even I can ride a bike!" sniggered David.

Hilda gritted her teeth and jumped back on the saddle. But as soon as she began to pedal, she lost control again and swerved into oncoming traffic. Cars with oblong headlights roared past on either side of her, honking angry horns.

"She can't ride for peanuts!" jeered a troll on a unicycle.

"She doesn't know how!" laughed a lindworm in a taxi.

Hilda gripped the handlebars until her knuckles went white. "Frida! David! Wait for me!" she cried, but Frida and David were so far ahead they could no longer hear her. The street rose up steeply in front of Hilda. She was still pedaling like crazy but her bicycle was beginning to slip backward.

Help me, thought Hilda, desperately ringing her bicycle bell. She tried to scream, but her throat was dry as dust and she could not make a sound. Trolberg Main Street was now almost vertical, stretching upwards into the clouds.

The bell fell off the unruly bike and clattered on the ground.

Then the grocery basket fell off.

Then the chain, the pedals and the wheels fell off. Still clutching her useless handlebars, Hilda slid down the tarmac slope all the way to the bottom of the street and out the city gate.

Hilda's teacher, Miss Hallgrim, was watching from the top of a bell tower.

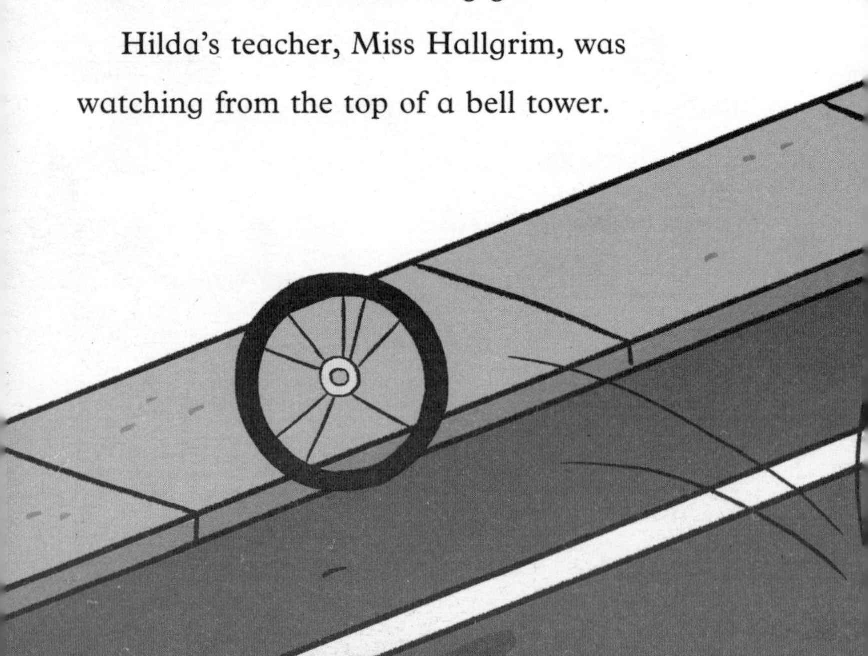

"Good riddance to bad riders!" she yelled.

"It's a *NO* from me!" roared Raven Leader.

The gates slammed shut, the sun dropped out of the sky and the snowcapped mountains echoed with a long, loud shriek of despair.

10

"Wake up, Hilda!" Someone was shaking her by the shoulders. "Hilda, wake up!"

Hilda opened her eyes and blinked. "David," she said. "You're supposed to be in the tent."

"I was," said David. "But I couldn't stay there. I just couldn't."

Hilda sat up. Her mind was foggy and her whole body ached from having been so tense for so long.

"As for you," said David, glancing up, "you should be ashamed of yourself."

Hilda rolled onto her back. The nightmare spirit hovered above her, greasy hair hanging down like dark curtains on either side of her pale face.

"Ashamed? *Moi?*" The spirit's tone was sarcastic, but there was also a note of uncertainty in her voice.

"Yes, you!" David shook his fist at the marra. "You're MY nightmare spirit and I won't have you giving nightmares to anyone else, do you hear? If you've got a nightmare, you bring it to ME and no one else."

The marra raked her hair with nervous fingers. "So, you're basically saying you want more nightmares."

"Exactly!" David grinned. "Tunnels. Rat kings. Salt lions. Trolls. Pile 'em high and bring 'em on. Just leave my friends alone!"

"Ugh." The nightmare spirit curled her lip. "You think you're so noble, don't you?"

"Not really," said David. "I was just bored of giving into fear. I thought I'd try facing it instead."

The nightmare spirit scowled at David.

David scowled back.

The clock on David's wall ticked loudly.

"You people disgust me," said the marra at last. *"Ooh, look at us, we're such good friends, we'd do anything for each other.* David, I have half a mind to haunt you every single night for the rest of your life, but as it turns out, it's no fun giving nightmares to people who ask for them." She shot a bitter glance at Hilda. "So yeah, whatever, I'm moving on. You three losers won't be hearing from me again."

With that, the nightmare spirit shrank to a wisp of airy thinness and disappeared through the keyhole.

The moment the marra was gone, David rolled his eyes, tipped sideways, and fainted right there in the middle of his bedroom carpet.

There was no more unpleasantness that night. Hilda and Frida splashed water on David's face until he was revived, then said goodnight and headed off down the drainpipe back to their tent. They climbed into their sleeping bags and fell into a sweet, dreamless sleep.

But when Hilda woke early next morning, she felt uneasy. She was pleased that David had begun to face his fears, but what about her? What about last night's bicycle nightmare, and the paralyzing fear that lay behind it?

"*Psst,*" Hilda whispered. "Frida, wake up!"

Frida groaned and rolled over. "What's the time?" she mumbled. "Is it morning?"

"Frida, I lied to David the other day, when we were buying cucumbers."

"Cucumbers? What? Who?"

"He asked why I didn't bring my new bike to the stores and I told him I didn't want to get it dirty, but that was a lie. The truth is, Frida, *I don't know how to ride a bike.*"

"I don't care," said Frida.

"I thought if I asked for a bike for my birthday, I would stop being scared of them. But now that I actually own a bike, I'm even more scared than before. What do you think I should do?"

"I think you should let me sleep." Frida ducked down into her sleeping bag and zipped it up from the inside.

"I'll tell you what I'm going to do," said Hilda. "I'm going to face my fear, like David did last night. I'm going to get my bike right now and I'm going to learn to ride it."

An exaggerated snoring sound came from Frida's sleeping bag. A quieter snoring sound came from one of Frida's socks, where Alfur was still sound asleep.

Hilda grabbed her adventuring satchel and trusty beret, crept out of the tent, and ran back home. She had never seen Trolberg this early in the morning. The stores were still closed and the streets were empty except for a few dog walkers. The air was crisp and fresh. A blackbird on a lamp post twittered cheerfully.

There on the bicycle rack outside Hilda's apartment block stood her brand-new birthday bike. The royal-blue frame sparkled in the morning sun and the chrome fittings gleamed.

Hilda took a deep breath. She took a key from a string around her neck and unlocked the bike.

Twig appeared at her bedroom window with his paws against the pane. As soon as he saw Hilda, he squeezed through the half-open window and made his way nimbly down the side of the building, leaping from sill to sill and down into her arms.

"Hello, boy," Hilda whispered. "Want to join me on an adventure?"

Twig sprinted around the bicycle rack seven times with his tail in the air.

Hilda smiled. "I'll take that as a yes."

She sat on the saddle, pressed the front pedal, cycled ten feet—and fell off! She got on. She fell off. She got on. She fell off. She got on. She fell off.

Twig was a sympathetic companion. Every time Hilda sprawled on the sidewalk, the faithful deer fox ran to her and nuzzled her face until she got up. After a dozen false starts, Hilda was grazed and teary-eyed, but she kept on doggedly picking herself up and trying again.

Hilda made her way past the library and downtown, where a man in a flat cap was piling newspapers onto a newsstand. He glanced up as Hilda approached, then winced as she crashed to the ground.

"Having trouble?" he asked, lifting the bike off Hilda's legs.

"Yes," she said, "but such is the life of an adventurer."

Hilda got to her feet and picked up her beret. As she replaced it on her head, she noticed the front page of the *Trolberg Tribune*. OM-NOM-NOM-NIVORE! the headline shrieked, and then in smaller type: BLACK HOUND GUZZLES PARKING ATTENDANT IN ONE GULP.

Hilda shuddered as she remembered being chased at Camp Sparrow. "They really need to catch that thing," she said.

"Easier said than done," said the newspaper man. "No one has any idea where it is, you see."

Hilda swallowed hard. "It's over there," she whispered.

The newspaper man chuckled.

"I'm serious." Hilda pointed. "It's right over there."

11

The Black Hound was at the far end of Trolberg Main Street, rambling along the sidewalk in the gray glow of dawn. Its deep chest tapered to a narrow waist. Its hindquarters were muscular and powerful. Its tail hung low with a slight upward curve toward the end.

Twig's hackles rose as the hound turned a corner and disappeared from sight.

"I'm going to follow it," said Hilda.

"Follow it?!" The newspaper man stared.

"Sure. If I can find out where that thing's lair is, maybe the police can catch it and stop it from eating anymore people."

Hilda opened her adventuring satchel and took out her sketchbook and pencil. She scribbled a message, tore it out, and impaled it on Twig's antlers.

GONE CYCLING. BACK IN TIME FOR BADGE CEREMONY XX

"Go home, boy," she said. "Give this to Mom."

Twig cocked his head on one side and looked up at her with bright black eyes.

"Don't worry about me," said Hilda. "I'll keep a safe distance, I promise."

Hilda pressed down on her front pedal and set off wobbling along the sidewalk. She rounded the corner, and there ahead of her was the hound, still slinking along in the shadows. It stopped to forage in a garbage bin, then carried on down Fredrik

Street toward the city gate.

Hilda passed four homeless house spirits on Fredrik Street alone. So strange, she thought. A few days ago, I had never seen a house spirit, and now I've seen tons of them.

She wanted to stop and talk to the banished spirits, but the hound was beginning to pick up its paws and bound along at a speedy pace. Hilda followed it through the gate and north toward the wilderness.

Sheep grazed. The river babbled. Blue pines waved their slender branches. Here on the left was a rowanberry bush and a patch of long grass perfect for making grass trumpets. There on the right was the railroad track with the desolate Steinharr (sea of stones) beyond. And here, just in front of her, was a pothole exactly the right size and shape to trap her front wheel and send her flying over the handlebars.

Hilda sat up and picked bits of gravel out of her palms. She realized with a jolt of excitement that this was the first time she had fallen off the bike in almost ten minutes. "I'm learning," she murmured to herself. "I'm finally getting better!"

She heaved her bike upright, jumped back onto the saddle, and pedaled like crazy. Her fear of bikes was gone and all that remained was the pure, fierce joy of cycling in the wilderness. With a song in her heart she whizzed past banks of celandine and roadside ditches thick with kingcups.

The Black Hound was far ahead. It kept disappearing over the crest of a hill or down in a dip. More than once Hilda thought she had lost it, only for it to reappear again much further on. Then all of a sudden, it veered off the street and trotted up a steep slope carpeted with saxifrage and giant rofflewort. There it stood at the top of the hill, silhouetted against a cloudless sky. It lifted its head, gave a mournful howl, then disappeared down the other side.

Hilda thought fast. She hoisted her bike into the middle of a giant rofflewort for safe keeping, and sprinted up the slope all the way to the top. But when

she reached the top of the hill and looked down, there was no sign at all of where the Black Hound had gone. Just the dark canopy of the Great Forest, stretching westwards as far as the eye could see.

Give up and go home, thought Hilda. That would be the sensible course of action. But then she remembered the headline in the *Trolberg Tribune*. What would that poor parking attendant want her to do? Keep going and locate the monster's lair, of course. Prevent any more of Trolberg's citizens being gobbled up for lunch.

Hilda ran down the hill into the Great Forest and very soon she was completely and utterly lost. A pine marten flashed past in pursuit of a hare. A crossbill wedged a fir cone into the crook of a tree and pecked the seeds out eagerly.

A ghost came swooping out of the shadows, light as thistledown. For a brief second its yellow eyes gazed into Hilda's soul, then it glided on past and disappeared among the iron pines.

Relax, Hilda told herself. A gray owl, nothing more.

On and on she wandered, deeper and deeper into the unknown. And then she saw something that made her heart leap. On a tree stump up ahead sat a little wooden man with a coconut-shaped head.

"Wood Man!" cried Hilda, running toward him. She had known him when she and her mom had lived in the wilderness. "Wood Man, I'm so happy to see you. How long has it been?"

The Wood Man turned his head and looked at Hilda with large expressionless eyes. "I don't know," he said. "I haven't been keeping track."

"Listen, Wood Man, I'm looking for a hound. Have you seen it? It's huge and black with bloodshot eyes and slobbering jaws, and it walks like this"—Hilda dropped to the ground and rambled along on all fours with her bottom in the air—"and it sounds like this"—Hilda crouched further down and gave a low, mournful howl—"and it ate a parking attendant yesterday so it's very important that we find its lair and tell the police—"

"Be quiet," said the Wood Man. "I'm trying to

concentrate here."

Hilda stopped. She noticed that the Wood Man was holding two playing cards close to his chest. She also noticed that he was not alone. Seven tiny elves were sitting with him in a circle, clutching two cards each and glaring up at Hilda in annoyance.

"Sorry," said Hilda. "I didn't see you there."

"We get that a lot," frowned a bearded elf.

"What are you playing?"

"Elf Poker," said the Wood Man. "Now stop talking. We'll be done soon."

"And then you'll help me find the—"

"Shush."

"The Black—"

"SHUSH!"

The bearded elf dealt three cards into the middle of the circle. "Four hares, seven oak leaves, King of acorns," he announced.

The elves took it in turns to place bets. Their expressions were blank. The Wood Man's expression was blankest of all.

The bearded elf dealt another card. "Duchess of oak leaves," he said, and there followed another round of betting.

"I've never understood the rules of Elf Poker," said Hilda. "I'm more of a Dragon Panic girl myself."

"SHUSH!" yelled all the players in unison as the bearded elf dealt a fifth card into the center.

Hilda shushed and sat down. She hugged her knees and took deep breaths of fresh wilderness air. It felt good to be back here after six long months in the big city. She had missed this tranquil life, full of simple pleasures and firm friendships.

"A pair of acorns against a forest flush," said the Wood Man. "Oh dear, I think I just lost something valuable."

"Really?" said Hilda. "What did you lose?"

"You," said the Wood Man.

"I'm sorry, did you say *me*?"

"Yes."

"You bet me in a poker game?"

"Yes."

Hilda frowned at the Wood Man, then down at the elves. "Alright then," she said. "Which of you little fellows is going to take me away? 'Cause I'd like to see you try, that's all!"

"Not them," the Wood Man sighed. "Him."

The Wood Man pointed to two trees in the shadows behind him, trees which on closer inspection turned out to be gigantic trunk-like legs. Hilda looked up, and gasped. There among the branches of the iron pine canopy loomed the furious face of a forest giant.

12

"How long are you going to keep me here?" Hilda demanded for the umpteenth time. "I'm supposed to be searching for the Black Hound's lair, you see. It's kind of urgent."

She was sitting in the hollow of a pine tree a hundred feet above the forest floor. In the hollow with her were various other treasures: a chessboard, a piano stool, books, records, three umbrellas, and a ukulele.

"Why didn't you see me at the card game?" the

forest giant demanded, also for the umpteenth time. "Why do you humans always overlook us? You wouldn't overlook an ancient giant, would you?"

"Of course not," said Hilda. "ancient giants are much big—" She broke off, not wanting to offend.

"Go on, say it!" the forest giant cried. "Ancient Giants are much bigger. And what does that make me, huh? A teeny-tiny, eensy-weensy, itsy-bitsy PYGMY GIANT, am I right? You're cruel to think it, girl, and you're even crueler to say it! What if I went on and on and on and on about how small YOU are? How would you like THAT? I can't even speak to you right now, I'm so angry. I can't even look at you. I can't even breathe the same air as you, that's how angry I am. GAH, I'm out of here!"

The giant stalked away in a huff and his colossal strides carried him out of sight in an instant.

Hilda crawled to the edge of the hollow and peered down. The nearest branch was more than ten feet below her. If she could get to that branch, she could probably climb the rest of the way down

the trunk. But that was the problem. If she jumped down from here, she was likely to break the branch or miss it completely. She was stuck.

Hilda imagined her mom reading and re-reading that vague message on Twig's antlers: GONE CYCLING. BACK IN TIME FOR BADGE CEREMONY. She imagined Mom arriving at the Scout Hall and sitting miserably through the ceremony with one eye on the door. She imagined her going out into the street afterwards, wringing her hands and shouting Hilda's name.

There would be a search, of course, but no one would ever find her bike inside the giant rofflewort or guess that she was being held hostage at the top of an iron pine in the middle of the Great Forest. Everyone would simply assume that she had been eaten by the Black Hound. Weeks, months, and years would pass, and every evening Mom would sit on the couch with Twig in her arms, weeping softly into his fur.

"This is all the Wood Man's fault," Hilda said

out loud. "I can't believe he BET me in a game. If I ever see him again, I'll knock that silly coconut of a head right off that weedy log of a body."

"Charming," said a doleful voice below her.

Hilda looked down and saw the Wood Man standing on a branch below her.

"You!" cried Hilda. "What are you doing here?"

"This and that," said the Wood Man, "I was hoping you'd help me reclaim some of my belongings."

"Wait a second, are you saying you lost me to that giant on purpose?"

"Of course." The Wood Man raised his arms. "You didn't think I'd go all in with two acorns when there was a Queen of hares in the river, did you?"

"No, I didn't think that," said Hilda, "because, one, I wasn't following the game, and two, I don't know what any of those words mean."

The Wood Man considered this. "If you like," he said at last, "I could lend you a book about Elf Poker."

"I . . . don't . . . want . . . a . . . book . . . about . . . POKER!" Hilda was struggling to keep calm.

"That forest giant is a mean poker player," the Wood Man said. "He's won lots of my stuff over the years. Last month, he won my ukulele . . ."

"I don't care."

"And my piano stool . . ."

"I DON'T CARE!"

"And my rope ladder . . ."

Hilda opened her mouth, then shut it again. She dove into the hollow and started searching through the giant's hoard. Right at the bottom she found what she was looking for—a good strong rope ladder with beechwood rungs.

She lowered it for the Wood Man and up he climbed, without a word of thanks. He walked past Hilda and gathered up his possessions: books, ukulele and a silver tiara.

"Was that tiara yours?" asked Hilda.

"I would prefer not to lie to you," said the Wood Man, placing it on his head. "Here, take these," he added, handing her a pair of ragged bellows.

A shadow fell across the hoard. There before

them, blocking the entrance to the iron pine hollow, was an enormous face.

"Look who we have here!" boomed the forest giant gleefully. "If it isn't my old friend the Wood Man, come to pay me a visit."

The Wood Man gazed back, expressionless.

The giant whooped and clicked his fingers. "Wood Man, Wood Man, bo-boodman! Banana-fanna, fo-foodman! Fee-fi, mo-moodman!"

"Stop that," the Wood Man muttered. "You're embarrassing yourself."

"I've caught a thieving Wood Man!" rapped the giant. "That man's my favorite food, man, when I'm in a manic mood, man!"

Hilda had heard enough. She lifted the bellows and squeezed them hard, blowing a cloud of dust into the giant's face. As the giant staggered backward, clutching his eyes, Hilda and the Wood Man leapt out of the hollow and onto the rope ladder.

"Stop, thieves!" roared the giant.

Hilda and the Wood Man scrambled down

the ladder hanging from the iron pine trunk, like startled, clumsy birds. The giant made a grab at them, but they managed to evade his fingers, scramble all the way to the ground and set off running across the forest floor.

The giant blinked and rubbed his eyes. "Scoundrels!" he yelled. "You wouldn't have robbed a true giant like this. GAH! Listen to me, calling them 'true giants'. Look what you've done to my self-esteem!"

Hilda and the Wood Man sprinted through the forest. It was a strange kind of chase because the giant kept overstepping them and had to double back.

"Villains!" roared the giant. "Imps! Rapscallions! If I was a real giant I'd grind your bones to make my bread. *Real giant?!* I didn't mean that! GAH!"

The Wood Man dropped his ukulele, books, and tiara in his hurry to escape.

"Oh no!" he cried. "My belongings! Mostly."

"Leave them!" shouted Hilda, grabbing his hand

and pulling him forward.

They ran on a few hundred yards and flung themselves under the gnarly roots of a bristlecone tree. They lay there in the dark hardly daring to breathe, while the giant blundered to and fro, searching for them.

A foul smell assailed Hilda's nostrils.

"Ew, Wood Man!" whispered Hilda. "This is a confined space. Control yourself."

"Me?" whispered the Wood Man. "I thought it was you."

Hilda took a tiny flashlight from her pocket and switched it on. The root system of the bristlecone tree extended much further and deeper than she had imagined. There were four-toed paw prints all over the earth and at the back of the cave lay the biggest pile of dog poop she had ever seen.

"Look," whispered Hilda. "I think we've found the Black Hound's lair."

13

As soon as they were sure that the forest giant had moved on, Hilda and the Wood Man wriggled out from their evil-smelling hiding place.

"What now?" said the Wood Man.

"Back to Trolberg, I guess," said Hilda, "to tell the police the precise location of the Black Hound's lair."

"And you know how to tell them that, do you?"

"No, I have no idea," Hilda admitted. She rummaged in her adventuring satchel and pulled out her sketchbook, and pencil. “Any chance you could write it down for me or draw a map or something?”

“Why would I do that?”

“To say sorry for losing me to a forest giant in a game of poker?”

“Alright.” The Wood Man took the sketchbook and began to draw. “Tell me, city girl,” he said, “do you miss the wilderness?”

“I thought I did,” said Hilda, “but after today I’m not so sure.”

The Wood Man drew a big X on his map and handed the sketchbook back. Hilda offered her hand for a farewell shake, but the Wood Man just stalked off through the trees.

Hilda took out her compass and held it gingerly in front of her. Half an hour later, to her surprise and delight, she emerged from the Great Forest and crested a hill overlooking the River Björg.

“Geronimo!” she cried as she rolled down the east side of the hill, reveling in the scent of crushed saxifrage.

"Bingo!" she shouted as she spotted a black handlebar poking out of a giant rofflewort.

"Trolberg, here I come!" she sang as she climbed onto her bicycle and headed for the city, stopping only to pick a bag full of rowanberries.

The Trolberg police were nowhere near as impressed or grateful as Hilda had anticipated. She had expected a bravery medal at the very least, but the officer at the desk just gazed at the Wood Man's map with a bemused expression, like a blobfish looking at a spelling test.

"The Trolberg police are no longer dealing with the hound case," he said. "The Safety Patrol are handling it now. They have a unit in every neighborhood of Trolberg."

"So give the map to the Safety Patrol."

The officer thought about this, then shook his head slowly. "No, I don't think that would work, miss. The Safety Patrol can't go to the Great Forest. They have no authority outside of Trolberg."

"So go there yourselves."

The officer considered this, then shook his head again. "I'm sorry, miss, but it's out of our hands. We are no longer dealing with the hound case."

Hilda banged her fist on the counter so hard that all the officer's papers and pens jumped into the air.

She barged out of the police station, climbed onto her bike, and pedaled off down the street. What was the point of risking life and limb to track down a monster, if the authorities were not willing to do their part?

The Gorrill Gardens bell tower struck two o'clock, along with all the other bells in the city. Hilda sped up. Only one hour to go until the start of the Sparrow Scouts Badge Ceremony.

She was determined to go to the ceremony and clap for Frida and David, but at the same time she was dreading it. She had earned a grand total of zero badges and Mom was about to discover the full extent of her daughter's feebleness.

As she neared home, Hilda saw something that made her stop and stare. A house spirit in white pajamas was being chased down a garden trail by an elderly woman with a broom.

"Get out!" shrieked the woman, slamming the garden gate. "And don't come back!"

The house spirit wore a floppy hat on its head

and a pair of round glasses on its enormous nose. It sat down on the street and sniffed loudly.

Hilda leaned her bike against the garden fence. "What's going on?" she said.

"He's a vandal!" snarled the woman.

"I didn't do anything," the house spirit muttered.

Hilda turned to the old woman. "Are you sure about what you saw?"

"Of course I'm sure." She waved her broom angrily. "I was having my usual nap after lunch when I was woken by the most dreadful racket, like someone was smashing up the kitchen. I came down to see what was going on, and there he was," —she jabbed the broom at the house spirit— "standing there in the middle of all the debris. He had ransacked the place, looking for something to steal. He must have gotten bored with all the stuff he had swiped over the years, because that was all over the floor as well."

Hilda turned to the house spirit. "Well?" she said.

The house spirit shrugged. "I don't know what

happened," he said. "One minute I was sitting in Nowhere Space, in my favorite armchair, then suddenly an earthquake struck."

"An earthquake?"

"Or a whirlwind."

"A whirlwind?"

"And the next thing I knew, I was standing in the kitchen surrounded by junk."

"A likely story!" snarled the old woman. She leaned over the fence and bashed the house spirit over the head with her broom.

"Don't do that!" cried Hilda. "I think he's telling the truth."

The old woman bashed Hilda over the head for good measure, then turned on her heel and marched back up the garden trail.

Hilda rubbed her head. She looked at the forlorn house spirit. "Do you know Tontu?" she asked.

"All house spirits are called Tontu," he replied. "And we talk to each other as little as possible. We despise each other through and through."

Hilda picked up her bike, said goodbye to the house spirit and went back home. She ran up the three flights of steps to her front door and let herself in. A heavenly aroma of ginger, nutmeg, and caraway seeds wafted over her.

"Hello!" she yelled. "Anyone home?"

Twig streaked into the hall like greased lightning and threw himself at her so hard she nearly fell over.

"Hello, darling!" Mom called from the kitchen. "Did you have a nice bike ride?"

Hilda went in and hugged her. "A little traumatic,"

she admitted, “but such is—”

“The life of an adventurer!” Mom chorused, smiling warmly. “I’m proud of you, Hilda. Now you’ll be able to add a Cycling Proficiency badge to your haul. Speaking of which, we need to get a move on if we want to be on time for the ceremony. Go and change into your Sparrow Scouts’ uniform, chop-chop. Your neckerchief slide is on the chest of drawers.”

Hilda poured the rowanberries from her satchel into the fruit bowl and walked to her room with a heavy heart. She could not bring herself to confess that she had not even earned her Camping badge. Mom would find out soon enough.

14

"Ladies and gentlemen, boys and girls, welcome to the Scout Hall for this, the ninety-third Badge Ceremony of the Trolberg Sparrow Scouts!"

Raven Leader was standing at the microphone in the middle of the stage. Sitting to one side was a tall, wiry man with a bushy beard and twinkling blue eyes. He wore a green safari jacket, khaki shorts, and big, black boots.

Raven Leader beamed. "Our special guest for today's ceremony is a naturalist, an explorer, and a bestselling author. Some of you will already be familiar with his books; *CAVES AND THEIR UNFRIENDLY OCCUPANTS, TUNNELS AND THEIR UNFRIENDLY OCCUPANTS* and *FORESTS AND THEIR UNFRIENDLY OCCUPANTS.* Please give a big round of applause for Mr. Emil K. Gammelplassen!"

Hilda gave a squeak of excitement and clapped until her hands hurt. She turned to look for Mom among the parents at the back of the hall. Mom caught her eye and gave her a thumbs up. They were both big Gammelplassen fans.

"Before our distinguished visitor makes his speech, we have some badges to present. As always, we begin with those who have earned the most badges. Frida, come on up!"

Frida gasped in fake surprise and made her way up onto the stage. Sitting in the front row, Hilda whooped and whistled, overjoyed at her friend's success.

"Frida has done extraordinarily well this year," said Raven Leader. "She has achieved her Fund-raising, Paddle Sports, Stonework, Circus

Skills, Young Entrepreneur, Emergency Aid, and Camping badges."

Frida shook hands with Emil Gammelplassen and staggered back to her seat, weighed down by all the new badges on her sash.

As Raven Leader called another high achiever to the stage, Hilda glanced down at the floor and noticed something strange—a tuft of blue fuzz poking out of a crack in the floorboards at her feet. She waited for the next round of applause before dropping to her knees. "Tontu, is that you?" she whispered.

"My savior." Tontu's voice dripped with sarcasm. "A ministering angel, with yet more delicious sandwiches for me to enjoy."

"Sorry about that night," Hilda whispered. "Something came up. Anyway, it's good to see you've found a piece of Nowhere Space to call your own."

It was David's turn to receive his badges. Hilda sat up and joined in the applause as her friend slouched up to the stage.

"David has done well this year," said Raven Leader. "He has earned his Choral Singing badge, his level two Swimming badge, his Camping badge, and his Friend to Insects badge!"

Claps and cheers echoed around the hall as David brushed a bug off his head and shook the great explorer's hand.

The ceremony continued with those who had earned three badges, then two, then one. Hilda felt a sudden pang of sorrow. There would be no gleaming badges for her this afternoon. No firm handshake. No word of congratulation from her hero.

The last of the badge-winners left the stage.

"And that," Raven Leader was saying, "brings us to the end of the presentations. Well done, all of you. Now our guest will make a speech."

Hilda glanced behind her and saw a range of emotions pass across Mom's face: first confusion, then shock and finally sadness. Their eyes met and

Hilda mouthed two words.

Sorry, Mom.

Emil Gammelplassen bounded to the front of the stage and took the microphone out of its holder. "Good afternoon, my friends!" His voice was loud and deep. "I am delighted to be with you today to celebrate your fine achievements. Although I must confess, I usually make it my aim to avoid cities as much as possible."

The audience laughed.

Emil Gammelplassen's blue eyes twinkled. "The wilderness!" he cried. "That's the place to be! That's the place that makes me feel truly alive!"

Me too, Hilda thought.

"I love to explore the great outdoors, armed with only a sketchbook and a stubby pencil."

"Me too," Hilda whispered.

"And when I'm far from home, completely and utterly lost, why, then I'm happier than ever!"

"Me too!" Hilda yelled out loud, then clapped a hand over her mouth and blushed bright red.

"I have trekked through forests," the explorer boomed. "I have climbed up mountains and skied down glaciers. On one memorable but uncomfortable occasion, I squatted in the belly of a giant rofflewort for three days and three nights, hiding from a family of unusually aggressive trolls."

At that moment, Mom came and sat on an empty chair next to Hilda. "Not a single badge!" she said in a loud whisper. "Not even the Camping badge?"

"I'm sorry, Mom." Hilda's eyes filled with tears. "I was unlucky."

"Unlucky?" whispered Mom. "I'm sorry to say this, Hilda, but maybe if you'd spent less time messing about with house spirits, you'd have had more time for badges." She tutted, stood up, and returned to her seat at the back of the hall.

Hilda put her chin in her hands. A tear rolled down her cheek. Mom's words had cut her deeply.

15

Up on the stage, Emil Gammelplassen was still in full flow. He had begun to recite a poem on the subject of adventure.

"*Sail to a shoreline where no one has been,*
Discover a grotto that no one has seen,
Ascend a mountain mired in snow
Or map dark tunnels deep below."

A sudden clunk came from the ceiling of the Scout Hall. The famous naturalist paused and glanced up uncertainly before continuing.

"You see that troll with two fierce heads?
Don't ever say die until you're dead.
You hear a ghost or wild elf?
There's nothing to fear but fear itself!"

Hilda looked up at the ceiling. There it was again, that clunking, scrabbling sound. What on earth could be up there?

"I have spoken long enough!" boomed Emil Gammelplassen. "Keep adventuring, my friends. Laugh, strive, explore, dream, and may the wind be always at your back!"

At that moment, Tontu sprang up through the crack in the floorboards and started tugging on Hilda's neckerchief, jabbering like a tizzybird. As for the sound in the ceiling, it was louder than ever.

"What's the matter?" Hilda hissed. "Tontu, do you know what's up there?"

But before Tontu could reply, something fell out of a ceiling panel and landed between Hilda and the stage. Screams and gasps erupted from the audience.

"IT'S THE BLACK HOUND!" screeched Raven Leader.

"Keep calm!" cried Emil Gammelplassen. "We have nothing to fear but fear itself!"

His words fell on deaf ears. Everyone except Gammelplassen and Hilda rushed toward the back of the hall, scrambling over each other in their hurry to escape.

The Black Hound swished its tail, licked its jaws, and advanced toward Hilda. Perhaps it remembered her as a source of delicious cucumber sandwiches, or perhaps it was still annoyed at not having been able to extract her from the bludbok tree. Either way, it was coming straight at her.

"Quick!" said Tontu, seizing Hilda's hand. "Come with me!"

The house spirit dragged her to a mousehole in the baseboard. He tightened his grip on her hand and gave a good hard yank. The Scout Hall swirled around their heads and collapsed in on them like a broken umbrella.

SHOOP!

Hilda staggered to her feet and looked around. The Scout Hall's Nowhere Space was empty, except for a few broken chairs and misplaced badges.

"No time to gawp!" cried Tontu. "We've got to get out of here."

The wobbly walls and floor shuddered as a huge black shape rushed up behind them, filling the space on every side. As the dark whirlwind flew toward them, Hilda and Tontu dove through a random portal and found themselves in an aisle of towering bookshelves.

"This is the Municipal Library," gasped Hilda.

"No time to read!" cried Tontu, sprinting along the aisle.

A moment later the Black Hound burst out from behind a storage heater in an explosion of broken chairs, trampled badges, and dusty books.

"In here!" yelled Tontu, diving behind a bookcase.

Hilda held on tight to Tontu's hand and let herself be dragged in and out of dozens of private houses and public buildings, via the baffling labyrinth of

Nowhere Space. The hound kept chasing, snapping its jaws at their heels.

One portal they went through felt strangely cold. The reason for that soon became clear. Hilda and Tontu fell out of a fridge onto a hard kitchen floor.

"*Ow!*" said Tontu. "I hurt my ankle."

Hilda jumped up and slammed the fridge door shut. "We can't stop now," she said. "That thing is still—"

WHUMP! The fridge door flew open again and the Black Hound tumbled out on top of them, scattering butter and clutter and sausages all over the floor.

"*Ouch!*" said Tontu. "Now I've hurt the other ankle."

Hilda wriggled out from underneath the hound. She grabbed a fruit bowl from the kitchen table and tipped it up in front of the slobbering beast. Rowanberries bounced and rolled.

The hound gobbled the berries in a few short

seconds, then advanced toward Hilda, growling menacingly.

All of a sudden, Hilda recognized her surroundings. “This is my house!” she exclaimed.

“Actually, it’s MY house.” A bald nisse slid in between Hilda and the hound, wielding a broom. “And I don’t allow hound dogs in the kitchen!”

The hound arched its back and stuck its muzzle right up close to Baldy’s face. It opened its jaws and a long pink tongue flopped out.

SLURP! The hound gave the house spirit a friendly lick on the face.

Baldy scowled, then a glint of recognition appeared in his eyes. “Jellybean?” he whispered.

“Huh?” said Hilda.

“Jellybean!” cried Baldy, flinging his arms around the Black Hound’s neck. “I haven’t seen you since you were a pup!”

16

The house spirit settled down on the couch surrounded by lime green cushions. Jellybean sat next to him, the top of his head squashed against the ceiling. Hilda and Tontu sat on the floor and listened to Baldy's story.

"I found Jellybean a long time ago," said Baldy, "when we were both little. He was lost, so I did what house spirits do with lost things. I took him home . . . I looked after him in secret for a while, but then my parents found him and took him from me. They said he was something called a barghest and that they would take him back to the mountains where he belonged. I never saw him again. I had no idea that he had come back to Trolberg to look for me. I don't hear much news in Nowhere Space, you see."

"I'm sorry to tell you this, but your pet is dangerous," said Hilda. "He swallowed a parking attendant in one gulp."

"Did he now?" Baldy reached up and bopped the Black Hound on the nose. "Bad Jellybean. Cough it up, please, right this second!"

Jellybean made a disgusting retching sound and vomited a parking attendant onto the living room carpet. The parking attendant took one look around and ran screaming from the apartment, still carrying her little book of parking tickets.

"This explains everything," said Hilda. "You taught Jellybean how to use Nowhere Space when he was a puppy, so this week he's been using it to move around the city. Trouble is, every time he charges through a nisse nest, he's so massive he takes everything with him. It's like a whirlwind coming through."

"So that's what happened!" cried Tontu. "My house-man assumed it was me that trashed the place."

Baldy chuckled and gave the barghest a big, sloppy kiss. "Have you been making a mess, Jellybean? You always were a messy pup!

Yes, you were! Yes, you were!"

"He's been hiding out in the Great Forest," said Hilda, "and in the woods near the campsite too. He's been just about everywhere."

"And now he's come home!" said Baldy with tears in his eyes.

Jellybean was not the only one who had come home. Hilda could hear footsteps on the stairs and the sound of the front door opening.

"Hilda!" Mom sounded desperate. "Hilda, are you here?"

Hilda ran out into the hall and gave her mother the biggest hug ever.

"Darling," said Mom. "I'm so glad you're safe. I lost sight of you in the Scout Hall, in all the chaos."

"I'm fine," said Hilda.

"Hilda, please forgive me," said Mom. "I was horrible to you at the Badge Ceremony, and I wish I could take it back. I know you always try your best at everything you do."

"That's OK," said Hilda. Right now she was

more worried about the barghest on the living room couch than about anything else.

"By the way," said Mom, "There's a very disturbed person shouting in the street. Soaking wet, and yelling something about jelly beans. Mr. Farmor on the ground floor has called the Safety Patrol."

Sure enough, the sound of distant sirens was already audible. "The Safety Patrol!" Hilda cried. "Why?"

"That woman needs help, Hilda. She wasn't in her right mind."

"But if the Safety Patrol come here, they'll find—"

"Find what, darling?"

"Find—" There was nothing for it but to tell the truth. "Find the barghest!"

Hilda talked fast, relaying to Mom the story of Jellybean exactly as she had heard it from Baldy.

"I see." Mom clutched a coat rack for support. "And where is this Jellybean creature now?"

"He's in the living room," said Hilda.

"He's sitting on the couch."

Mom walked to the door and peeked into the living room. She went really pale but managed to stay upright.

The sirens of the Safety Patrol were closer now. Jellybean perked up his ears. His eyes grew big and round.

"There, there," said Baldy. "Keep calm, boy."

But keeping calm was the last thing on Jellybean's mind. He leapt off the couch and made a run for it, galumphing through the open front door and down the stairs.

"Jellybean!" yelled Baldy. "Come back!"

Hilda and Baldy ran to the window and looked out. Jellybean was standing in the middle of the street, surrounded by vans emblazoned with the words SAFETY PATROL. He was barking and whimpering and his ears were turned back in fear.

One of the hound hunters fired a net gun at the frightened barghest. It missed, but the sound of the gun made Jellybean rear up in panic. The other

hunters raised their net guns in unison.

"Somebody, do something!" cried Baldy. "They're going to catch him."

Hilda suddenly remembered her conversation at the police station. "Mom, you've got to help us," she said. "We need to get Jellybean out of the city."

"Out of the city? Why?"

"The Safety Patrol only have authority within Trolberg. If we can get Jellybean outside the city walls, they can't touch him."

Mom hesitated for a moment, then grabbed her car keys. "Alright, come on," she said.

Hilda, Tontu, Baldy, and Mom raced down to the first floor, three steps at a time, and barged out into the street. Eleven uniformed, hound hunters turned and stared at them.

Mom ran to the car and jumped into the driver's seat. Hilda, Tontu, and Baldy piled in too. The engine squealed, the wheels spun, and the car shot down the driveway in reverse.

Baldy wound down the window and leaned out.

"HEY, Jellybean!" he yelled. "Follow the car, boy! Come on!"

The barghest took a flying leap over the hound hunters and onto the street behind Mom's car. The hunters jumped back into their vans. The sirens started up again.

"They're coming after us!" yelled Mom, stepping hard on the gas. "Fasten your seat belts and hold onto your hats!"

17

Past the grocer's shop they raced, then past the church and the marketplace. Mom's car was in the lead, closely followed by Jellybean, closely followed by the hound hunters. Other drivers heard the sirens and pulled their cars to the side of the street to get out of the way of the speeding convoy.

"Turn left here, Mom," Hilda said. "We can cross the river at Ulvik Bridge."

Mom flicked the steering wheel a little to the right and then made a hard left. The tires squealed, the back swung out, and the car drifted perfectly into the turn.

"Woah!" gasped Hilda. "Where did you learn to do THAT?"

Mom flashed her a grin.

"Nice to know I can still surprise you," she said.

The train station and the library flew past in a blur of brick and concrete. Hilda turned and saw that Jellybean was gaining on the car. His nose was almost touching the back bumper.

"Where are we?" cried Baldy.

"Fredrik Street!" yelled Hilda. "The city gate is really near now. In fact, I think I can see— WOAH!"

The barghest made a mighty forward leap and landed on the front of the car, denting the hood, and completely blocking the windshield.

"Jellybean, get out of the way!" cried Hilda. "Mom, slow down!"

"I can't!" shrieked Mom. "The brakes aren't working!"

Baldy turned to Tontu. "Take my hand!" he said.

"We need to work together."

"It's too dangerous!" Tontu hissed. "Remember the Ehrenfest Paradox!"

The car careered off the street, smashed through a fence, and zoomed down a slope. Hilda stuck her head out of the window to see where they were going and immediately she wished she hadn't. "Mom!" she screamed. "We're heading straight for the city wall! We're going to crash!

"Take my hand, Tontu!" Baldy repeated. "It's now or never!"

The house spirits interlaced their fingers and plunged their hands down in between the car seats. SHOOP! In an instant the car and all its contents were sucked away into Nowhere Space.

Hilda's ears popped and she felt a sharp pain in her chest. Outdoor Nowhere Space was nothing like Indoor Nowhere Space. Here there were no wobble-walled tunnels or cozy furnishings. It was dank, dark, and cavernous. Worst of all, it was airless. Hilda winced and squirmed, unable to breathe.

POOSH! In a sudden burst of light and color, the car shot back out of Nowhere Space. It landed on two wheels, bounced a few times, and came to a stop in a muddy field. Hilda sucked in a delicious lungful of air.

The occupants of the car sat in silence. They inhaled deeply and blinked at each other in astonishment.

"What on earth just happened?" gasped Mom. "Did we drive through the wall?"

"Of course not," said Tontu. "That would be impossible."

"Where's Baldy?" cried Hilda. "And where's Jellybean?"

Tontu sighed. "They're probably miles away."

"What? Why aren't they with us?"

"It's time I explained the Ehrenfest Paradox," said Tontu. "Imagine a disk—a plate or a frisbee or something. Imagine the disk is spinning around at the speed of light."

"OK."

"Now imagine that there are five baby mice sitting on the edge of the spinning disc—and that the disc gets karate-chopped by a giant."

"OK."

"Do you think those mice will all end up in the same place?"

"No. I suppose not."

"Well, that's life," said Tontu cheerfully. "Looks like your home is without a nisse now . . ."

That evening Hilda lay on the couch and read the rest of *FORESTS AND THEIR UNFRIENDLY OCCUPANTS*. Twig lay curled up by the fire and Mom sat sewing in an armchair.

"Finished," said Hilda, closing the book. "Not as good as his book on caves, but almost."

"I've finished too," said Mom, coming to sit beside her. "I've made something for you, Hilda."

"What is it?"

"Well," said Mom, "I've been thinking about all the Sparrow Scouts badges that it's possible to get, and I realized that there's no badge for helping a homeless house spirit."

"Of course there isn't," said Hilda. "That would be silly."

"And there's no badge for tracking a barghest through the wilderness to rescue a parking attendant that's been eaten."

"That would also be a pointless badge," said Hilda. "No one except me would ever earn it."

"I suppose that's my point." Mom reached over and patted Hilda's hand. "You are unique, Hilda, and not a single Sparrow Scouts badge exists for any of the wonderful things you do. So I took the liberty of making you a badge myself."

Mom held up Hilda's Sparrow Scouts' sweater. On the top of the sleeve near the shoulder was a heart-shaped badge containing a wonkily-stitched picture of Hilda and her mom.

"This is the Love badge," said Mom, her voice shaking with emotion. "It shows to the whole world that you're the kindest, bravest, most selfless girl a mother ever had."

Oh no, Hilda thought to herself. What an embarrassing badge. No one at Sparrow Scouts must ever, ever see it.

"Thanks, Mom!" She kissed her on the cheek. "You're the best."

"*Ahem*," said a voice. "Sorry to interrupt this beautiful moment, but your drinks are ready."

Tontu popped out from between the couch cushions, a steaming mug of hot chocolate in each hand. Hilda and Mom took one each.

Alfur popped out after Tontu and scurried up Hilda's arm into her ear, carrying a tiny notepad and pencil. "This is the beginning of a golden age of elf exploration," he enthused. "Just think of all the missing paperwork that may have fallen down into Nowhere Space!"

Hilda smiled to herself. It was the beginning of a golden age of exploration for her, as well. Now that she had conquered her fear of cycling, there was no limit to the places she might go and the adventures she might have.

"Mom," said Hilda, as an exciting idea struck her. "Do you think the tent will fit in my bike basket?"

Mom thought, then shook her head. "No, it's too big," she said, "but I guess you could split it between three bikes—yours, Frida's, and David's."

Hilda's face lit up in an enormous grin. "Yes, that might work," she said, her heart racing with excitement. "That might work very well indeed."

Enjoyed *Hilda and the Nowhere Space?*
Then don't miss the fourth book in the series . . .

HILDA AND THE TIME WORM

Catch up with your favorite blue-haired adventurer as she meets new creatures and faces new perils in the latest instalment of Hilda tales.

Can't wait to get your hands on it?
Here's a sneak peek just for you . . .

1

Wind blew. Woffs flew. Deep, crisp snow lay all around. At the Sparrow Scout stall in Trolberg marketplace, a little girl with blue hair leaned over a steaming cauldron, sticking her tongue out.

Hilda always stuck her tongue out when she was cooking. It helped her concentrate. Her wooden spoon delved into the corners of the pot, swirling and churning its invisible depths: onion and mushroom, potato and carrot, mountain garlic, and fresh kintoki ginger.

The Sparrow Scout soup stall needed real teamwork. Hilda was on stirring duty, David was on chopping duty, Twig was on tail-chasing duty,

and Frida was on recipe management. It was her great-great grandmother's secret recipe and Frida was determined that it be followed to the letter.

"Hurry up, everyone," said Frida. "The customers will be arriving soon."

"Yes, chop-chop, David," said Hilda, giggling at her own pun.

To the left of the stall stood the Sonstansil tree, its branches heavy with large, white buds. In a land full of unusual trees, this tree was even more unusual than most. At school that morning, Hilda had researched it and had written some amazing facts in her topic book.

1. The buds of the Sonstansil tree appear on the first day of the Winter Festival.
2. They open gradually during the three nights of the festival.
3. When the last bud opens, the flowers begin to glow in the dark, an event known in Trolberg as the Big Glow.
4. The morning after the Big Glow, everybody throws parties and gives presents.

CHAPTER ONE

Hilda had never seen the Big Glow before, and she was very excited.

"Hey, Witch Girl," said a mean voice nearby. "Is it true that you caused last week's snowstorm? I heard that you rode a broomstick into the heart of a snowstorm and that you talked to a weather spirit and that you made it snow on Trolberg more than it has ever snowed before."

Trevor, the class bully, was standing on a mound of snow to the right of the Sparrow Scouts stall.

Hilda put down her wooden spoon and scowled at him. "It wasn't a broomstick, Trevor, it was a thunderbird. And it wasn't one weather spirit, it was a whole crowd of them. And I didn't start the snow, I stopped it. If it wasn't for me, the whole city would be completely buried by now. You can thank me if you like."

"Alright." Trevor picked up a handful of snow and packed it tight between his hands. "Here's my way of saying thank you."

"Go away, Trevor," stammered David.

"Bug Boy!" said Trevor. "I didn't see you there. Look everyone, Bug Boy's crying!"

"I'm not crying," said David. "I've been chopping onions!"

Kelly and Anders, two of Trevor's naughtiest friends, appeared beside him. They too were holding snowballs.

"Careful," said Frida. "The soup is boiling hot."

"Boiling hot?" Trevor grinned. "Don't worry, we'll cool it down for you."

A volley of snowballs sailed through the air. Hilda, David and Frida dived for cover under the table. Soup splashed. Peppers rolled. The SPECIAL SPARROW SCOUT SOUP sign clattered to the ground. Twig's fluffy tail puffed up to twice its normal size.

"Come out, come out, wherever you are!" came Kelly's singsong voice.

"They're seriously appreciating the coziness under that table!" giggled Anders.

"David, Frida, listen to me," Hilda hissed. "On the count of three, we jump up, grab a vegetable—a squashy, rotten one, if possible—and we throw it at those meanies as hard as we can."

"Really?" David sounded unsure. "I thought

SPA
OWSCOUT

that hiding under here was working out pretty well so far."

"We can't let them bully us," said Hilda. "So, on the count of three. One..." She wrapped her scarf around the lower half of her face. "Two..." She crouched on the balls of her feet. "THREE!"

With a ferocious battle cry, the three friends leaped up. Hilda grabbed a tomato. Frida grabbed a potato. David, his eyes tight shut, grabbed a mushroom. They lifted their vegetables, ready to strike.

Trevor and his gang were nowhere to be seen. Instead, a broad-shouldered man and a young woman were standing in front of the stall. Both of them wore the caped brown and yellow uniforms of the Trolberg Safety Patrol.

A button mushroom pinged off the big man's nose.

"David, open your eyes," hissed Frida. "You just hit a Safety Patrol officer on the nose with a mushroom."

"It's fine," said the big man, though the expression on his face said it wasn't fine at all.

"Now, which of you two girls is Hilda?"

"I am," said Hilda.

"Allow me to introduce myself. I am Erik Ahlberg, commander of Trolberg Safety Patrol. This is Gerda Gustav, my deputy."

Hilda gulped. "Have I...done something?"

"Yes, you have," said Ahlberg, twirling his thin moustache. "You have won our very first ASPECT!"

Gerda let off a party popper, making David jump.

Hilda stared at the officers through tumbling confetti. "First what?"

"ASPECT," said Gerda. "Annual Safety Patrol Essay Contest Trophy."

Frida squealed, making David jump again. "The essay contest!" she cried. "Don't you remember, Hilda, in class last week Miss Hallgrim made us all write an essay on the topic 'Trolls: Perils and Preparedness.' It sounds like your essay won!"

Hilda did remember. She had written her essay about something that happened to her in the wilderness before she and Mum moved to Trolberg. She had lost track of time while sketching a troll rock and ended up having to run away from a very angry troll with a bell on its nose. As it turned out, she need not have worried. All the troll wanted was to get rid of the bell and return her sketchbook.

"You'll receive your trophy at a ceremony tomorrow morning," Ahlberg continued. "After that, you join us on an inspection of the city's troll defenses."

"I can't," said Hilda. "I have school tomorrow."

"Principal Magnusson has already given permission," smiled Gerda. "Commander Ahlberg will lead a special school assembly, then we'll take off from the playground in a zeppelin."

"What's a zeppelin?"

"A dirigible," said Gerda.

"What's a dirigible?"

"An airship," said Gerda. "The perfect vehicle for an adventurer."

Hilda's heart leapt. "Count me in," she said.

How much can you remember from **Hilda and the Nowhere Space**? Answer these fiendish quiz questions to find out!

1. **What color scarf was Baldy wearing?**
2. **Name one of the chief scout's scary campfire songs.**
3. **How many Sparrow Scout badges did David earn?**
4. **What did Frida use to tie the marra to the bedpost?**
5. **What is the Black Hound's real name?**

Answers: 1. Stoat Girl, 2. Gorrill Gardens Bell Tower 3. Any 5 of– Burping Bugtrap, Giant Roffilewort (aka Hide-and-Seek Flower), gyrating geraniums, scurvy grass, nila grass, blue nettle, moss with leg, 4. Sigrid Spensting, 5. Trollslayer

ABOUT THE CREATORS

LUKE PEARSON

Luke Pearson has fast become one of the leading talents of the UK comics scene, garnering rave reviews from *The Guardian*, *The New York Times* and *The New Yorker*, amongst others. He was the winner of the British Young People's Comic Awards in 2012 and 2018. He has worked as a storyboard artist on the cult classic show *Adventure Time* and currently lives in Nottingham, UK.

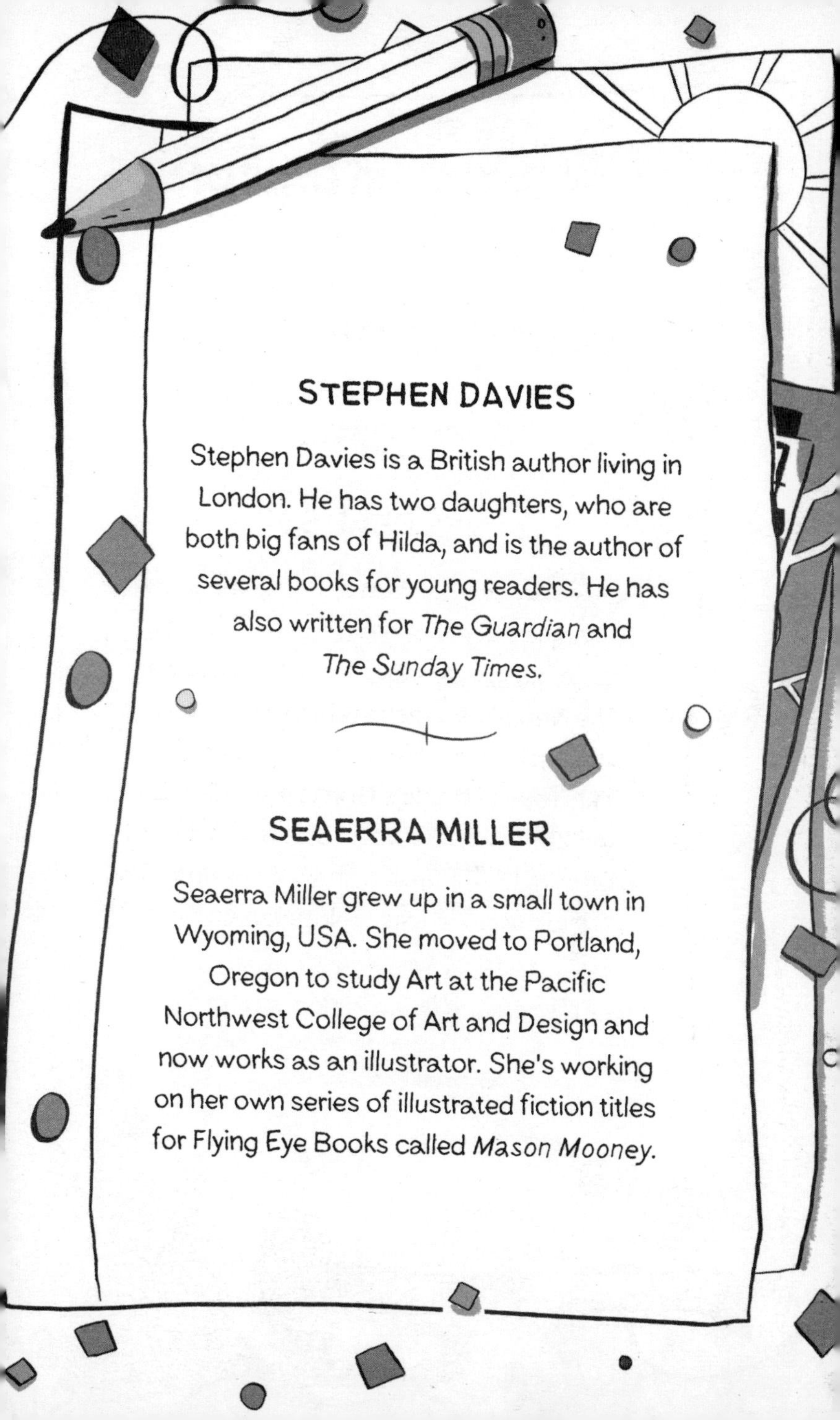

STEPHEN DAVIES

Stephen Davies is a British author living in London. He has two daughters, who are both big fans of Hilda, and is the author of several books for young readers. He has also written for *The Guardian* and *The Sunday Times.*

SEAERRA MILLER

Seaerra Miller grew up in a small town in Wyoming, USA. She moved to Portland, Oregon to study Art at the Pacific Northwest College of Art and Design and now works as an illustrator. She's working on her own series of illustrated fiction titles for Flying Eye Books called *Mason Mooney.*

PRAISE FOR THE HILDA COMICS

"Pearson has found a lovely new way to dramatise childhood demons, while also making you long for your own cruise down the fjords."
The New Yorker

"Plain smart and moving. John Stanley's Little Lulu meets Miyazaki."
Oscar award-winning Director Guillermo Del Toro

"Hilda is a curious, intelligent, and adventure-seeking protagonist."
School Library Journal

"The art is as whimsical as the protagonist, and the bright colours enhance this comic book's magical realistic effect."
The Horn Book Review

" Luke Pearson's Hildafolk series mixes humour, mystery and fantasy into a superb piece of escapism for young and old alike."
Broken Frontier

PRAISE FOR THE HILDA FICTION

"A fun and pacey adventure combining a contemporary heroine with a gentle mythological element."
BookTrust

"Want to take the kids on a great adventure? Hilda is the one!"
The Great British Bookworm

"I have loved Hilda since the Hildafolk graphic novels, and now the full-length novels are just as good (maybe better)!"
Mango Bubbles

"Dynamic cartoon art brings the book to life, Hilda's bravery is an inspiration, and the world's details–the giant she chats with, the rabbit-riding elf army–will pull readers in."
Publishers Weekly

"The Hilda books are already beloved favourites of many kids; the Netflix series and these chapter books are likely to get her even more fans."
The Beat

WATCH

HILDA

ON NETFLIX!

She's a fearless blue-haired girl who travels from her home in a vast magical wilderness, full of elves and giants, to the bustling city of Trolberg. There she meets new friends and mysterious creatures who are stranger —and more dangerous—than she ever expected.

Season 1 now streaming on Netflix.
Season 2 coming in 2020.

COLLECT ALL THE BOOKS IN THE HILDA SERIES . . .

FICTION BOOKS

Written by Stephen Davies

Hilda and the Hidden People
Hilda and the Great Parade
Hilda and the Nowhere Space
Hilda and the Time Worm
Hilda and the Ghost Ship
Hilda and the White Woff

GRAPHIC NOVELS

Written and illustrated by Luke Pearson

Hilda and the Troll
Hilda and the Midnight Giant
Hilda and the Bird Parade
Hilda and the Black Hound
Hilda and the Stone Forest
Hilda and the Mountain King

Discover more of Hilda's world at
www.hildabooks.com